T

Accidental

Wife

ERICA RIDLEY

Four left for war.
One stayed home.
The battle is just beginning...

Chapter One

June 1816
London, England

Lawrence Pembroke, Duke of Ravenwood, could not wait to escape the Palace of Westminster. As usual, the "short" meeting of the House of Lords had not begun until four in the afternoon, because most of the lords present could not be expected to rise from their beds until at least two of the clock.

Ravenwood, however, had been up since dawn. He favored neither drunkards nor dancing, and was not at all pleased that what had been meant to be an intelligent, practical debate on the efficacy of recoinage for greater post-war stabilization of currency had deteriorated once again into speculation about Princess Charlotte's recent marriage and gleeful gossip about the appearance of a maskless Miss Katherine Ross at one of the Duke of Lambley's masquerade parties.

Lambley got away with such chicanery because he was a duke. He was not only the very reason why Parliament could not possibly be called to order at a more reasonable hour, but the blasted man was garrulously and delightedly recounting tale's of Miss Ross's exploits. Miss Katherine Ross was Lambley's hoyden cousin, who had apparently staged her stunt to entice other frivolous aristocrats to attend some equally frivolous upcoming crush.

Ravenwood would not be attending. Ever. Besides a visceral dislike of both crowds and parties, he disdained any behavior that cheapened one's title or one's integrity.

He wouldn't even be at the Palace of Westminster at a quarter 'til midnight if he didn't hold his responsibilities as a duke and a member of Parliament in the utmost respect. He, at least, would uphold his duty to England despite certain capricious lordlings wasting valuable time with idle gossip.

And he would leave here before midnight if humanly possible. His sister had begged him to stop by for a late supper after the meeting, and Ravenwood had given his word.

He rose to his feet. "I propose we form a Coinage Committee to investigate options and propose not only a course of action, but also a schedule in which to achieve it."

Conversation halted as dozens of faces swung in his direction.

Ravenwood kept his tone imperious, his face a blank mask despite his pounding heart. He disliked being stared at even more than he disliked crowded rooms, but duty came first. The House of Lords needed a nanny, but tonight it must make do with Ravenwood. Experience had taught him that the most expedient way to achieve a goal was to undertake it oneself.

Very well.

"Anyone interested in joining the fiduciary committee should arrive two hours prior to our next meeting. Until a chair can be formally named, I shall head the effort in the interim." He sent his cool, imperious gaze about the chamber. "Unless one of you would like to volunteer for the position?"

Of course they would not. The handful of lords with enough intelligence and conviction to join such a committee was bright enough not to volunteer to manage it. The more foolish, indolent lords could be trusted to still be abed at the appointed hour, sleeping off another night of revelry.

So be it.

As soon as the meeting was adjourned, Ravenwood stalked from the Court of Requests and out into the chill night air. Only once he was seated inside his stately coach-and-four did he allow himself a small sigh of relief at finally achieving a moment's peace.

Six more weeks. That was all. Parliament would disperse in July and would not resume until the following November.

Thank God. He sagged against the squab. Nothing sapped his energy and his spirits as efficiently as being forced to interact with crowds of people whom he could neither comprehend nor corral.

Which was perhaps ironic, given he was currently en route to his sister Amelia's town house.

Lady Amelia was the epitome of a woman unable to be corralled, but he did at least *comprehend* her. He not only valued her sharp mind and managing ways, but also quite missed her presence in his household, now that she was married to Lord Sheffield.

Ravenwood hadn't even realized how much he had missed her until he'd received her invitation to dinner.

He had always maintained a silent, retiring nature, but without his sister about to put her nose where it didn't belong, the only words spoken to him at home these days were *Yes, Your Grace* or *Perhaps the blue waistcoat today?*

Ravenwood straightened his cravat. He was very much looking forward to an hour or two in the company of someone who didn't want or expect anything of him. Amelia was one of the few people in the world who thought of him as her brother, the person, rather than His Grace, the duke.

When his coach-and-four pulled in front of the Sheffield town house, Ravenwood alighted from the carriage in haste.

His sister would not be surprised by his extremely late arrival—nothing surprised Lady Amelia—but Ravenwood's stomach had been growling since half eight, and it was now past midnight.

The butler opened the front door before Ravenwood was halfway up the walk, and ushered him from the foyer to the dining room with no delay.

Lady Amelia all but clapped her hands with glee at his arrival. "Lovely to see you, brother. Your salmon will be served momentarily." She shot a pointed look over her shoulder. "I told you he'd arrive, if you would suffer the least bit of patience."

Given that her husband, Lord Sheffield, had never once displayed an ounce of impatience, Ravenwood could only surmise that Lady Amelia had invited other guests to her table.

Guests whose presence would once again force him to resume the role of His Grace, the duke. Delightful. He turned to greet them.

A surprised smile tugged at his lips.

Major Blackpool and his wife Daphne leapt to their feet. Or rose awkwardly, in Daphne's case. She was partway through her first pregnancy, and still getting used to navigating her new dimensions.

"Good to see you," Ravenwood said gruffly. And so it was.

With them, there was no need to put on airs. Their company was a pleasure. Bartholomew Blackpool had been one of his bosom friends since they were children.

Much had happened since then. Ravenwood's parents had died while he was a schoolboy at Eton. The French Revolution had been raging for years, and had taken a turn for the worse right around the time they'd all left Cambridge.

When Blackpool and a few others had joined the Army to fight Napoleon, Ravenwood had not been able to join them. Indeed, he had initially been jealous.

From the moment he'd inherited his title, every breath, every moment, had been dedicated to the dukedom. To being the sort of man his parents would have wanted him to be. To being a duke that would have made them proud.

And that meant rigid adherence to gentlemanly conduct. Protecting the title and the estate. Staying home. Leaving battles and regimentals to freer men.

But the reality of war had soon become clear.

Major Blackpool had returned home not in glory, but delirious with pain. He'd lost his leg and his brother on the battlefield. He wouldn't be alive at all if another friend hadn't risked his own life to drag the injured man to safety.

Ravenwood swallowed. If he had been present that day, might he have been able to save his friends from tragedy? Or might he have been the one never to return, leaving his lifeblood and his father's cherished title to trickle into nothing upon the battlefield?

Now was not the time to dwell on dark thoughts. It was a happy surprise indeed to be able to spend the evening with close friends.

Before he could ask Daphne how she was faring or what plans they had for the baby, Ravenwood's sister forcibly tugged him toward a third party, whom he hadn't initially noticed due to his excitement to see the others.

His posture tightened at the sight of a pretty young lady with glossy blond hair, sparkling blue eyes, and a quick smile.

Miss Katherine Ross. Cousin to the infamous Duke of Lambley. Hoyden extraordinaire.

Ravenwood narrowed his eyes at his sister.

It was a truth universally acknowledged that Lady Amelia loved her brother dearly. And that she was an unrepentant busybody of the first order.

He would not put any scheme past his sister. Including a misguided attempt to matchmake her brother with a long-legged, laughing-eyed woman that he could not possibly abide. Ravenwood frowned at Miss Ross in distaste.

Lady Amelia barreled on, as if the sudden return of Ravenwood's icy public demeanor was of no consequence. "Katherine, it is my absolute pleasure to present His Grace, the Duke of Ravenwood. Ravenwood, please allow me to present Miss Katherine Ross. She is cousin to the Duke of Lambley."

"We've met," Ravenwood answered coldly. He detested being forced to converse with anyone who flouted propriety.

Miss Ross gazed back, unperturbed.

Ignoring society's conventions no doubt had led directly to her still unwed state, despite her high ranked connections and sparkling blue eyes. Ravenwood frowned. It would take far more than a pretty face to turn his head.

He had nothing but respect for the other individuals at the table. Every one of them consistently put duty above all other concerns.

The beautiful and brazen Miss Ross, on the other hand, had apparently spent the prior evening courting the edge of impropriety at one of her cousin's masquerade ball.

A few months ago, she had provided shelter during Daphne's courtship with Blackpool, however, which was no doubt how she had earned everyone else's blessing. Humph. Tolerable enough manners on that occasion, Ravenwood supposed, but hardly refined enough to tempt *him*. He preferred the company of people who could be expected to conform to society's rules.

Indeed, he would have chosen to sit at the opposite end of the table from Miss Ross, except the only vacant seat belonged to Lord Sheffield. All other chairs were taken. He stiffened his spine. There was nothing to do but accept the only empty place.

With his habitual mask of formal hauteur firmly in place, Ravenwood took the seat beside Miss Ross. His long-practiced indifference to those beneath a duke's notice allowed him to sip a much-needed glass of wine whilst cataloguing what could be made of the situation.

Familiar sweetness coated his tongue. He froze. Not just any wine—his favorite port. No doubt, then. His sister was absolutely up to her usual tricks.

He arched a brow at her.

She gave him a bland smile and blinked in wide-eyed innocence.

Dread soured Ravenwood's wine.

He and Miss Ross were opposites in every way. Ravenwood took pride in his lineage, his title, his comportment. In being an exemplary peer of honor and good breeding.

Miss Ross, on the other hand, had no such compunctions about…anything at all. If the recent scandal sheets were any indication, she had no respect for her time, her reputation, or her standing in society. She delighted in disrupting the status quo.

Which was no doubt why his obvious disapproval of her antics had no effect on her sunny smile. She was perfectly happy living her life precisely how she pleased.

Ravenwood's shoulders relaxed. He suspected that even Lady Amelia would have difficulty influencing a woman as infamously headstrong as Miss Ross.

Which, along with the Blackpools' presence at the table, suggested this was perhaps not a matchmaking ambush after all.

Knowing his sister, however, it was still an ambush. The question was why.

"How may I be of service?" he asked without preamble. He addressed the question to Major Blackpool, as he was the least likely to prevaricate in his reply.

Blackpool gestured toward his wife.

Daphne immediately blushed. "I wish you wouldn't

assume even friends don't dine with you unless they desire a favor. It makes it even worse on the occasions when you're right."

Ravenwood granted her a smile that he did not feel.

He liked Daphne. They *were* friends. But the truth of the matter was, since the moment he'd inherited the dukedom, virtually no one sought an audience with him unless they wished him to use his title for their benefit.

On most occasions, he was happy to use his influence to help others.

On other occasions, he simply wanted to enjoy a moment as a human being, not as someone else's stepping-stone.

Footmen rushed forward bearing steaming trays of fragrant delicacies, as if Lady Amelia's kitchen had synchronized their clocks with the timing of the parliamentary meeting.

From Amelia, he would expect nothing less. However, he had also expected her to uphold their childhood bargain of never forcing him into awkward social situations unawares.

Hours spent arguing with and wrangling the House of Lords were bad enough. He did not need a relaxing evening turned into more of the same.

"I have had a long day and a long night," he said to Daphne. "I am hungry and out of sorts. I am aware my sister has been helping support your charities. If you require a financial donation for one of your causes, the answer is yes. May we eat now?"

Daphne's gaze darted toward Miss Ross. *Not* Lady Amelia.

Ravenwood turned to Miss Ross in dismay. "Is this gathering *your* doing, Miss Ross?"

"Not this one," she answered cheerfully as she picked up her spoon. "I try not to organize anything with less than a hundred attendees. But you're right on the mark. While your financial contribution is always welcome, this time Daphne is aiming even bigger. She would like to auction art for charity. My antiquities museum is the perfect venue, both for displaying the objects as well as for hosting a large number of attendees. The date is Saturday next, at eight in the evening. It has the makings of a perfect crush."

Ravenwood held back a grimace. It did sound like a perfect crush. Horrid. "Presumably Daphne will handle distributing the funds to the appropriate parties, and Lady Amelia will handle the invitations and the auction itself. I fail to see my role in the scheme."

Miss Ross licked her rosy lips. "You are the bait."

He recoiled. His tone was of the same frigid disdain that could silence the House of Lords in the space of a breath. "Explain."

Miss Ross's blue eyes twinkled at him from over her glass of wine. "You needn't scowl so. I promise you'll survive with your reputation intact. In fact, we're counting on it."

We. He turned his glare toward his sister.

Lady Amelia nodded enthusiastically. "Your presence at the soirée—"

"I thought it was an auction."

"It must be both, if we're to attract *everyone*. Most of the upper classes don't care a button about auctions—and they care even less about donating their largess to charitable causes. They do, however, care very much about keeping up appearances, and would be loath to miss a gala with the reclusive Duke of Ravenwood himself in attendance."

"My shadow will make the evening a success?" he asked sarcastically. Blast.

It was true, of course. And one of the many reasons he hated crowds. His mere presence always made them larger.

"Your attendance will attract...others." Miss Ross leaned back in her chair, her pretty face free of worry. "Your large donation, delivered before all and sundry, will open their pocketbooks."

"Why not Lambley?" Ravenwood suggested. There had to be an alternative. "Your cousin is a duke, financially sound, *and* popular. Is his schedule too full to fit another soiree?"

Miss Ross waved her hand. "Of course my cousin will be there. Lambley would never miss a party. Which is precisely why his presence is unlikely to cause a stir. Lambley's notoriety is more likely to generate gossip than altruism. You, however, are someone the sheep affect to imitate."

Ravenwood clenched his teeth. If Miss Ross's goal was to sweeten him up, she was failing tremendously—and was undoubtedly enjoying every moment of it. The "sheep" she referred to were the upper classes. His peers.

She might think eschewing decorum and proper respect made her a free spirit, some sort of modern woman.

In truth, it simply made her unpalatable.

He was not, however, an unfair or unfeeling man. Far from it. Daphne's charitable causes always improved the lives of some underserved portion of the population, and Ravenwood would not allow his distaste for Miss Ross's lack of restraint to deter him from doing his part. As a duke, his first responsibility was to England.

His second responsibility was to his own peace and happiness.

"I will attend the auction." He looked down his nose at Miss Ross. "I will bid high, I will encourage others to do the same, and then I will take my leave. Once my duty is done, our paths will not cross again. Are my terms clear?"

Lady Amelia gasped. "*Ravenwood—*"

"Your delightful presence will be deeply missed from that day forward," Miss Ross said drolly, neither chastened nor flustered by his disapproval. Her lips quirked as she lowered her gaze to her glass of wine.

Ravenwood's jaw tightened. His cut had not insulted

her. Displeasing Ravenwood was likely the highlight of her evening. Miss Ross reveled in walking the line between respectable and fast. He could not tear his gaze away.

One night, he reminded himself. He would see her briefly from across the room—and then never see her again.

He couldn't wait.

Chapter Two

Miss Katherine Ross grasped the thin, liver-spotted hands of her Great-Aunt Havens and gaily twirled the older woman about the salon of the antiquities museum. "Isn't this *fun*, Aunt? Guests will arrive in less than an hour!"

Aunt Havens' smile was as instant and as exuberant as a babe's. Her eyes, however, did not light with understanding. "Are we having a party? Where are we?"

"This is my museum, Aunt. See all the glass displays atop those white columns? Those are the *objets d'art* Daphne will be auctioning for charity. She claims the cunning wooden animals inside them were carved by a *pirate*."

"A pirate!" Aunt Havens gasped in delight.

The same reaction she'd had the three previous times Kate had relayed this same bit of information.

No matter. Kate kissed her aunt's wrinkled cheek and led her to a comfortable chair with a direct view of the entrance.

Hopefully Aunt Havens would stop wandering off to the storage rooms this time. Every time she tried to "help" organize an event, another priceless artifact tumbled off its shelf.

Kate patted her narrow shoulder. "Relax right here,

Aunt. I'm going to help Daphne for a moment. Whistle if you need me."

"Whistling is not at all ladylike," Aunt Havens said sternly. "Don't engage in such antics once the Duke of Ravenwood is here, or he's liable to give you the cut direct in the middle of your own museum."

Kate's shoulders sagged with relief. No more vacant answers. Aunt Havens was back. She even recalled Kate's many complaints about the Frost King—the irreverent moniker Kate had once given him after he'd attended a ball and refused to dance with anyone.

She grinned to herself. Ravenwood might be a staid, emotionless, ice-in-his-veins stick-in-the-mud, but all that could be forgiven because Aunt Havens had *remembered* him.

Then again, despite his aloofness, the Duke of Ravenwood was handsome as sin. Who could forget wide shoulders and piercing green eyes like his?

Kate linked her arm with her aunt's. Aunt Havens' moments of confusion were brief, but Kate couldn't help but worry. Sometimes a month or two might go by without incident, and then other times Aunt Havens couldn't seem to grasp the conversational thread from one moment to the next.

Nights like tonight. When all Kate wanted was to share the joy of success with the sole close family member she had left. She leaned her head against her aunt's shoulder.

It was unfair. When Aunt Havens had opened her home and her heart to an orphaned little girl all those years ago, she hadn't just become a mother figure in Kate's life. Aunt Havens had become Kate's confidante, her conscience. Her best friend.

She straightened her spine. It was good to see Aunt Havens' eyes alight with wit and intelligence again. Whatever those moments of confusion had been, they were gone now. Aunt Havens was fine. She would *stay* fine. The two of them were a force to be reckoned with.

Starting with this charity soiree.

Kate clasped her hands to her chest and feasted her eyes upon the remade salon. Most of her precious antiquities were tucked safely into crates inside the back rooms, but a few carefully selected pieces were still on display.

With any luck, this gala would be a rousing success for Daphne's charity *and* Kate's museum.

She had spent days and weeks agonizing over which pieces would pique the most interest, which pedestals would display them to best light. If antiquities museums were not the preferred nighttime haunt of the fashionable set, well, Kate would simply have to change their minds.

The museum doors pushed open and a gaggle of Kate's artistic friends rushed in, talking excitedly. She rushed forward to greet them.

It was vital that the struggling artists be here tonight. They had donated most of the paintings, woodwork, and lavish costumes on display for the auction. This was likely to be their one chance to witness a high-priced auction and realize the true value of their maligned and under appreciated talent.

Yet to make that happen, Kate had to ensure their presence would not send the Upper Ten Thousand fleeing home before a single penny had been raised.

Although it pained her to do so, she had no choice but to usher each cluster of her lower-class friends up the stairs and out of the way. She told them they were fortunate. The balcony railing would provide them a bird's eye view of the proceedings.

They knew the truth. They didn't argue or take offense.

Kate's fingers clenched at her inability to make the *beau monde* accept talented artists like her friends simply because they were born from the wrong bloodlines.

Being near enough to spy bald spots atop moneyed roués was as close to equality as any of them ever expected to get. They were *happy* to be here.

"Don't spit on anyone," she teased before turning toward the winding staircase to intercept the next batch of guests.

"What about your Frost King?" Miss Nottingworth, a talented seamstress, teased back.

Kate gave an exaggerated shudder despite the quickening of her pulse. "He's not mine, thank heavens. I pity the future duchess who spends her wedding night suffering frostbite."

She slipped back down the steps to the sound of her friends' laughter.

While she did indeed suspect Ravenwood's touch to be capable of turning anything to ice, the mere thought of lovemaking did not send her a fit of the vapors, as it did so many of the useless debutantes gathering below.

What Kate dreaded was not the physical act, but marriage itself. The loss of her freedom. The requirement to bear children. The probability she or her child would not survive the ordeal. Kate's fingers grew cold. The very thought paralyzed her limbs with dread and sent her into a panic.

Many of her earliest memories were of her Aunt Havens' drawn face when she'd returned from a midwifery visit only to report one or both of the patients had not survived the birth.

Uncle Havens had been a parson. Each time, he would comfort his wife as best he could, then prepare for the funerals.

The sight of tiny coffins even smaller than Kate herself had been more than enough to convince her never to take such a risk.

As she'd grown older, as the cemeteries became crowded, her resolve had only strengthened. Losing one's own life would be terrible enough. Losing a child…unthinkable.

Kate shivered. She might fantasize about knowing

passion, but she did not need or want the trappings that came with it. She was perfectly happy to remain both a spinster and a virgin for the rest of her days.

Another reason why her artist friends loved to tease her. Many were not confined by the same rules and expectations. A few of them were married, but most took their pleasures when and how they pleased. They used scandalous devices like sponges or French letters to prevent conception.

Kate's sensibilities should have been shocked by such unseemly behavior. Instead, she was deeply jealous of their freedom. Of the ability to connect with others without forethought or consequence.

As a lady, choosing not to bear children meant never marrying at all. She sighed. Sometimes she wished *she* were made of ice. Then maybe her fate wouldn't seem so lonely.

For the moment, however, Daphne's auction deserved Kate's full attention. Streams of eager faces spilled through the front doors and into the receiving salon.

A grin spread across Kate's face as she stepped into the milieu.

She loved this. The noise of excited conversations, the clash of a hundred perfumes, the whirl of colors as expensive silks and painted faces sparkled beneath the light of dozens of chandeliers. She drew a deep breath as energy sang through her veins.

Within the space of a couple hours, Daphne's charity auction was a roaring success. The crème de la crème were having *fun* in an antiquities museum. *Kate's* antiquities museum. It was perfect. Champagne flowed. Bids soared. Her friends watching overhead were openmouthed and awestruck at the exorbitant prices their hard work was fetching. Aunt Havens was laughing with Daphne and her husband.

Kate's heart thundered with joy. Nights like this made her feel like she could do anything, be anyone she desired. The world was hers.

She clutched her hands to her chest and smiled at the whirling crush. What else might she accomplish if she put her mind to it? 'Twould be splendid if she could get the art-and-theatre crowd and the *beau monde* not only under the same roof, but actually interacting. Perhaps not like *peers*, but at least...like *people*.

A thought struck her. The *ton* loved to be entertained. They just didn't realize how much of an effect their patronage—or lack thereof—truly had.

Kate could spread awareness, much like Daphne was doing, except Kate's goal would be to entice the wealthier set to become more active patrons of the arts. Anyone could spare a few coins to sponsor the tutelage of a protégé. What Society matron wouldn't wish to boast that she'd "discovered" London's newest rising star?

The entertainment district would become richer in every sense. Artists and actors could focus on their craft instead of finding their next meal. And the *beau monde*, as spectators, would reap the benefit of their generosity.

Kate forced herself to push the tantalizing idea aside. At least for tonight.

Right now she needed to concentrate on flawlessly executing the charity event. Perhaps she could even lay the foundation for her future event by spending an extra moment with the faces she recognized as performers in past musicales, or those whose box was never vacant during a theatre performance.

Practically bubbling with excitement and good cheer, Kate made her way through the crowded salon. She gave a personal word of welcome to everyone she passed, teasing them all to return soon for a glimpse of the antiquities even their money could not buy. Mentioning favorite operas, favorite violinists to the aficionados who shared her passions.

A self-deprecating smile teased her lips. She could be more than charming when she wished. So could the *ton*.

With them both on their best behavior, the evening was positively magical.

Until she caught sight of high cheekbones. Chestnut hair. Strong shoulders.

The devilishly handsome Duke of Ravenwood stood back from the crowd, almost in the shadows, but there was no hiding a form that tall. A body that muscular. A scowl that dark.

Annoyance itched beneath her skin. A charity ball was clearly too gauche for someone as high in the instep as Ravenwood, but did he have to glower from his perch like a gargoyle in a waistcoat?

Not that his frosty arrogance discouraged the eyes of every woman in the salon from turning his way. For a duke, everything was easy. He probably took his passion wherever he pleased. If he ever had any passion.

She was reminding herself that she was not to let him ruffle her feathers, when his hooded green eyes met hers— and just as quickly glanced away.

Her mouth fell open. Was he truly going to stand inside her museum and pretend not to see her?

She took a step forward.

He turned his back and slipped into the shadows.

Of all the—Kate curled her fingers into fists. He might be the silent prince of the *ton* but he would *not* cut her right in the middle of her own museum. Ice King or not.

She sniffed.

He wished to avoid her? Too late now. He could melt into whichever corner he liked, but no one knew this museum as well as Kate. He would not cut her again. Her heart banged as she stalked through the crowd. He could be as uppity as he liked in his domain, but tonight he had walked into hers.

She found him in moments, standing beside the open door to the storage cellar as if he were entitled to poke his aristocratic nose anywhere he pleased, simply because he'd been born with a title.

Well, he might be the Duke of Ravenwood, but he wasn't lord of her museum. She'd built it from the ground up. Her unmarried status made it hers and hers alone.

Which meant she had every right to throw him out on his ear if he dared to insult her between these walls. After all, *she'd* invited *him*.

She stormed over with a ferocious smile. "Looking for the powder room, are we?"

He started in surprise—or at least, she thought he might have done—and then turned to face her in the slowest, haughtiest way imaginable. "The only thing I'm looking for is a respite from all the noise."

The "noise", as he put it, was the proof that her long weeks of planning and preparation had been worth every effort.

Of course His Grace wouldn't approve.

"By all means," she said as she brushed past him, "step into my lair. Be warned, there's more dust on these shelves than Ravenwood House sees in a year."

She strode into the storage area with her head high, pleased to have had the last word. His Highness would never follow her into such a lowly chamber.

Giddiness filled her. She had turned her back on him and walked away. Given the Duke of Ravenwood the cut direct. A laugh bubbled at her lips. Her friends would never believe this!

"You have never seen the inside of Ravenwood House," came a deep voice from right behind her. "Nor are you likely to."

She gasped and spun around, heart hammering.

He'd left his precious *ton* to follow her into storage quarters? Was he *mad*?

"Not be invited to Ravenwood House?" She arched a brow and tried to calm her pulse. "Be a gentleman and pass me your handkerchief. I fear I may weep."

His cool eyes didn't leave hers. "Come to think of it, I rarely see you at any society events. I've only seen your name in scandal sheets. Why is that?"

"Because you don't go to society events," she snapped.

He tilted his head to concede the point.

Good. She crossed her arms. If he wasn't already aware, she would hate having to explain to him that she was rarely asked to attend any of the "respectable" balls anymore. While she'd never done anything scandalous enough to permanently ruin her reputation, her friendships with the art and theatre crowd tainted her by association.

If she were a man, perhaps her motley friends wouldn't have mattered. Lord Byron managed to be a poet and a baron. Brummell managed to be both a dandy and a debtor.

For women, it was different. If one were an actress, the assumption was that she was also a whore. And if she were not an actress, but merely a woman who both enjoyed the performances and befriended the entertainers?

Well. She hadn't flinched when her Almack's voucher was revoked. She certainly wasn't going to cry about the Duke of Ravenwood acknowledging her lower status.

The opposite, in fact. His unexpected pursuit of her into the storage area filled Kate with a giddy sense of unreality. Part of her was picturing herself telling her friends about her close encounter with the Frost King, and the other part of herself wondered if they'd even believe her.

A prideful man as high-in-the-instep as the lofty Duke of Ravenwood, shadowed amongst dusty wooden crates and towering shelves? Unthinkable!

Even here, surrounded by row after row of her painstakingly collected antiquities, the insufferable man looked more imperious than ever. More handsome. More unreachable.

His broad shoulders and tense frame seemed to fill the overstuffed aisle, making her feel for the first time as if she were not in her prized treasure room, but rather a wayward maiden who'd wandered into *his* domain.

She glared at him for daring to take her sense of owner-ship from her with his mere presence.

His eyes glittered back from beneath his dark chestnut brows.

He neither smiled nor frowned. As was his wont. Ravenwood was infamous for staring coolly out of those inscrutable emerald eyes, with no indication upon those firm lips and square jaw as to what he might be thinking. She had spent weeks trying to figure him out. Months.

Kate straightened her spine and tried to match his indifference with her own.

Let him see how immune she was to his arrogance and cold beauty. If she wanted a statue of Adonis, she knew where to find one. She already had one, in fact—packed away against the back wall. She didn't need Ravenwood towering over her, judging her. Dismissing her.

She jerked her gaze away from him. The charity gala needed her concentration. Now that she was in the storage area, she might as well make something of it. But Aunt Havens had been in here earlier, "organizing" the collection…which always made it that much harder for anything to be found.

As Kate scanned the shelves in search of the Greek pottery she'd hoped to put on display after tonight's gala, every prickling inch of her skin was hyper aware of Ravenwood's unflinching gaze. Her usually steady fingers trembled as she reached for a squat wooden box tucked away upon one of the tallest shelves.

"Let me help," came his deep voice from immediately behind her.

She jumped and flailed her arms. The preternaturally silent man had managed to startle her yet again, causing her to grasp the shelving to keep her balance.

It didn't work.

Rather, *she* stayed upright—but the overpacked shelves

wobbled just enough to send the items on the topmost shelf tumbling right at them.

A blown glass flower. A porcelain bust. And Aunt Havens' misplaced pail of water.

Kate grabbed the bust and swung it onto the closest shelf.

Ravenwood rescued the glass flower.

The falling bucket splashed over them, dousing his wide chest and pristine cravat with cold water.

His impenetrable eyes met hers.

Kate swallowed. Her pulse hammered wildly. Words would not form.

He ought to look ridiculous. An uppity duke, clutching a glass flower, his neckcloth dripping as if he'd been caught in a summer rain.

The opposite was true. With his chestnut curls awry and his cravat plastered to his chest, the typically standoffish duke looked...*approachable*. Handsome. Dangerous.

She touched her fingertips to his cravat. "You're wet."

"You're observant." Against all odds, his mouth curved into a wry smile.

She froze in place, her palm against the heat of his chest, her startled eyes locked on the curve of his lips.

Had she ever seen him smile before? Heaven help her, he was gorgeous. That slow, self-deprecating smile transformed him from a princely statue to someone kissable. Desirable. Someone she absolutely should not be touching.

Fire, not ice.

She snatched her hand from his chest and jerked away—only for her slippered feet to skid out from under her on the water-slick floor.

He caught her to him, preventing her fall.

Her arms tightened about him reflexively before she realized her mistake. Er, mistakes. She was alone with the Duke of Ravenwood, her silk bodice plastered against his dripping wet chest.

And part of her didn't want to let go.

She tried to breathe. His muscles were firm and hot beneath his snugly tailored coat sleeves. Her damp bosom trapped between his heartbeat and hers.

His hooded green eyes were no longer as unreadable as they'd been a few moments earlier. They were focused on her parted lips. The lips she couldn't help but lick in anticipation.

He lowered his head toward hers…as the storage room door swung open.

Chapter Three

Ravenwood released Miss Ross from his arms, his heart pounding in trepidation.

It was already too late.

An older woman stood in the open doorway, blinking owlishly at them from a pale, angular face.

"Oh, thank heavens." Miss Ross all but sagged back into his arms in obvious relief. "It's just Aunt Havens."

Ravenwood stiffened. From what he had always gathered, aunts happening across an unchaperoned niece in the arms of a duke generally put one at distinct risk for a leg shackle.

He couldn't risk Miss Ross becoming his *duchess*, for God's sake.

She was intriguing and beautiful, but tempting curves and kissable lips were not the traits he most desired. No matter what his traitorous body might have thought when he'd given into temptation and pulled her into his arms.

He knew precisely what sort of woman would make the perfect wife and a wonderful duchess, and Miss Ross unquestionably did not fit his requirements.

When he married, it would be for his dukedom...and for love.

Or at least, that had been his plan until a few moments

ago.

However, Mrs. Havens had yet to sound the alarm. Or do much of anything besides stare at them, with her back to the noise from the gala and Ravenwood's freedom in the palm of her hand.

"She's frowning because she can be slightly addled at times, not because she intends to compromise us," Miss Ross whispered. "It's going to be all right."

Relief coursed through him.

His moment of weakness, of madness, was nothing more than that. A flight of fancy. It wasn't like he had *actually* kissed her.

Mrs. Havens had done them a favor by interrupting.

He tried to calm his racing heart. Miss Ross's ability to drive him mad with both distaste and desire did not deserve to be dwelled upon any longer.

Thank God they wouldn't be compromised. If they could not be in each other's company without arguing—or kissing—then they would simply take care to avoid each other's company.

Indeed, it was past time for Ravenwood to select a proper duchess. If he had already taken a wife, he would never have made the terrible mistake of a horrifically incompatible woman like Miss Ross.

He required someone of moral restraint, of unimpeachable reputation, of soft words and a gentle heart. A duchess who would command the unflagging respect of the entire *ton*. Once he took a wife, he would no longer be tempted by the likes of Miss Ross.

He forced himself to drag his gaze away from the pretty flush on Miss Ross's cheeks...and the sight of her tongue as she licked her lower lip.

No matter how badly he'd longed to escape the crowded salon, he should never have followed her into the storage area. Her goading was far less dangerous than the temptation of her kisses.

But then, who would imagine he could ever be tempted?

"There's no trouble here, Aunt." Miss Ross grabbed one of the dusty cloths covering the many crates and placed it atop the puddle on the floor. "We're just attending to a slight mishap."

"Why was a pail of water perched at the edge of a shelf to begin with?" he growled beneath his breath.

Miss Ross's blue eyes sparked up at him from beneath dusky lashes. "'Tis my museum, not yours. I'll store my possessions wherever I please."

"Did I leave my bucket on the floor?" came a querulous voice from the doorway.

Addled sometimes. He swallowed in sudden understanding. Miss Ross wasn't the beautiful, shallow creature he'd believed her to be. Her fiery glare hadn't been because she was cross with Ravenwood, but because she wished to protect her aunt from censure. He appreciated such a noble streak.

"Go back to the others," Miss Ross called over her shoulder. "I'll find you in a moment."

Ravenwood's entire body tensed as he waited to see whether Mrs. Havens would follow such a directive without asking what her niece was doing alone with a strange man in the first place.

To his relief, Mrs. Havens nodded as if this were a perfectly normal request. "Make haste if you could, please. Daphne has questions about the pink vases and Lambley says we're running out of champagne."

Ravenwood blinked at the mundane query.

Miss Ross had been correct. Everything was going to be all right. All they had to do was slip back into the salon before anyone else noticed them missing and then life would continue as planned.

The hardest part would be explaining why his cravat looked like he'd dropped it in bathwater.

As Mrs. Havens turned to close the door, her voice

floated back to them. "No, you'll have to wait for the champagne. Kate needs a private moment with a young man before she can join us."

Miss Ross flushed pink and sucked in a breath.

Ravenwood covered his face with his hand.

The storage door swung back open with enough force to rattle its hinges.

"Ravenwood?" spluttered the Duke of Lambley in disbelief. "Why are you skulking about with my cousin?"

"A fine accusation, coming from the likes of you," Ravenwood returned icily.

Lambley's more illicit parties were legendary for their hedonism. They were also precisely the wrong comparison to make whilst explaining why Ravenwood was alone with Miss Ross.

Mrs. Havens clasped her hands to her chest and fixed her nephew with a worried gaze. "Is something wrong, dear?"

"Ravenwood is about to ask my cousin for her hand in marriage right this very moment, that's what's wrong." Lambley stalked forward with his hands clenched into fists.

Miss Ross rushed forward. "Cousin, wait. It's not what you think!"

Lambley drew up short, his posture relaxing. "Please tell me there's a reasonable explanation."

For a moment—a brief, glorious moment—Ravenwood let himself believe that he would be able to exit this museum the same way he had entered it: a bachelor.

Then dozens of familiar faces swarmed the open doorway in shock and delight.

"What is it?"

"Lambley nearly engaged in fisticuffs with the Duke of Ravenwood!"

"A brawl? In a museum?"

"The Duke of Ravenwood has compromised Miss Ross!"

"Can you imagine her as a duchess?"

"Can you imagine Ravenwood compromising someone? His blood isn't made of ice after all!"

"A tryst, at a charity gala! Can there be anything more vulgar?"

"Must not have wanted him, though. Looks like she tossed her drink right in his face."

"Not want a duchy? Are you mad? That's a lover's quarrel, that is. She wanted to be more than a mistress, but he had his sainted image to uphold."

Ravenwood was clenching his jaw so tight he feared his teeth would grind to dust. His "sainted" image had been one of his prized possessions. An achievement of which he'd had every right to be proud.

In eight-and-twenty years, he'd never once given Society a reason to view his manners and his bearing with anything less than absolute respect.

In less than a quarter hour, he'd managed to tarnish *two* reputations. All because he'd ducked into a quiet room for a much needed respite from this very crowd.

He slowly turned toward Miss Ross, expecting to find her prostrate with mortification. Or perhaps smug with satisfaction, if the gossips were right about every woman's innate desire to become a duchess.

Miss Ross didn't look delighted at her unexpected new fortune. She looked like she was going to cry.

Devil take it.

Ravenwood's spine snapped into its habitual commanding posture. A sudden betrothal was the last thing either of them had planned, but becoming the new Duchess of Ravenwood was hardly the end of the world. For someone like her, 'twould be a giant step forward.

"Miss Ross." He forced himself to voice the dreaded words that had now become inevitable. "Would you do me the great honor—"

"It's no honor," she muttered back, glaring at his wet

shoes. "This is a nightmare for both of us."

Well. At least she acknowledged the truth. Ravenwood grabbed her hand and turned toward the jostling spectators. "She said yes!"

She dug her fingernails into his skin. "I didn't say yes. You didn't finish your sentence."

"Do you want this to become even more of a farce than it already is?" he asked through clenched teeth, forcing himself not to grab her. "If that bucket hadn't been there—"

"If you hadn't followed me somewhere you certainly didn't belong—"

"If you hadn't forced me into attending this ridiculous gala—"

"If you didn't have such a large stick up your arse—"

"If you could act like a lady for just once in your flighty, spoiled little life—"

"Congratulations," Lambley boomed. He yanked Miss Ross to safety before Ravenwood could throttle her for making a horrible situation even worse. "You may call upon us tomorrow to work out the details."

Ravenwood allowed his mask of ducal impenetrability to engulf him, cloaking his frustration behind an emotionless façade.

He inclined his head toward Lambley. The bounder was right. Duty before all else. He would not lower himself to arguing again. Not now, not tomorrow, not even when that pretty termagant became his wife.

Duty first. Nothing else mattered.

Not even his own happiness.

Chapter Four

Kate trudged into her Egyptian themed parlor and threw herself into the carved wooden chair across from her Aunt Havens.

The sun streamed merrily through the tall, rectangular windows on this beautiful June day, yet Kate gazed about her favorite room of the townhouse without her usual joy and satisfaction.

This was *her* townhouse. *Her* parlor. *Her* carefully themed rooms, decorated with minute accuracy down to the hue of the paint and the stitching on the chair cushions.

It had taken Kate her entire adult life to coax her Mayfair townhouse from an empty skeleton into a home she could be proud of. Each room a living replica of a moment in history. Each item purchased using the modest sum she'd inherited when her parents had died far too young.

Not only would she be expected to leave it all behind after the wedding—it wouldn't even belong to *her* anymore.

As soon as the marriage contract was signed and the ceremony completed, everything Kate had dedicated her purposefully spinsterish life to building would immediately become sole property of the Duke of Ravenwood.

She wished she'd thrown the bucket at him on purpose.

"How can you sit there and embroider on a day like

this?" she groused to her aunt.

Kate frowned. Perhaps Aunt Havens had the right of it. Heaven knew what she'd be "allowed" to do once they were under Ravenwood's thumb. This might be her last chance to run out and spend every penny she owned.

Not that she would. Ravenwood might not even let her keep her purchases. How was Kate to know what a duke might do? Especially a duke as notoriously cold and severe as Ravenwood. She drew in a shaky breath. Selling off her treasures would break her heart worse than never owning them in the first place.

Aunt Havens lowered her embroidery to her lap and peered at Kate. "Is he a nice man? Might he make you happy?"

Kate's shoulders sagged as some of the tension seeped from them. Aunt Havens was perfectly herself today, thank God. Kate needed her.

The two of them had been through so much. They'd lost homes, they'd lost all their loved ones, but they'd never lost each other.

Since the day Kate had been orphaned, she had confided all her fears and secrets to her aunt. She wouldn't be able to survive the upcoming changes without her aunt's advice, support, and unconditional love. Together, they could get through anything.

Including this.

"He's...respectable," she hedged in response to her aunt's question. Ravenwood was also handsome and self-righteous and proper and maddening. He turned her thoughts upside-down. "Or at least he *was* respectable, until my cousin's buffoonery made everyone jump to completely unfounded conclusions."

Aunt Havens tilted her head. "Lambley merely wished to protect you."

"I know." Kate leaned her head back against the chair and threw her arm over her eyes.

For all his rakish ways, Lambley would choose dueling pistols at dawn over the thought of someone taking advantage of his innocent cousin Kate.

And that was the jest, wasn't it? She *was* innocent in that sense. The moment with Ravenwood had been disappointingly innocent. She was a "fallen" woman who had never even been kissed. And was too terrified to bear children, for fear of losing them. Even for a husband who looked like Adonis.

She pulled herself up into a seated position. "I cannot be a duchess, Aunt. I don't want a husband at all."

Aunt Havens frowned. "You have no choice."

"We'll make each other miserable," Kate insisted. The quickening of her pulse meant nothing. She could not possibly marry him, for she couldn't perform *any* of her wifely duties. "He'll expect a sweet, proper, docile wife. I'm none of those things."

"Then you'll have to change. He's a duke. He has a right to expect those qualities."

Aunt Havens was right. Of course she was right. But Kate couldn't help a stab of resentment that becoming a duchess meant she had to stop being *Kate*.

"Why can't I expect things, too?" Kate's fingers clenched in frustration. Pricks of heat stung her eyes.

"You ought not to worry. He will take care of you." Aunt Havens picked up her embroidery. "It is his responsibility to provide for you in every way, from this day forward. Think of all the resources you'll have."

"I don't want his money. I have my own money." Or at least she used to. Very soon, even her museum would belong to her husband. Who would she be then? "I don't need anything from him, and I'd prefer he didn't require anything of me. I'd rather live in infamy than marry a man who only wants to change me."

Aunt Havens didn't respond.

Kate frowned. It wasn't unusual for her aunt to sit in

silence if she felt Kate was simply being dramatic, but the threat of not following through with the wedding should have warranted *some* sort of reply.

A soft snore escaped Aunt Havens' mouth.

Indecision paralyzed Kate. This was the fifth time in as many months that Aunt Havens had fallen asleep during daylight hours, right in the middle of doing something else.

Part of her wanted to let her aunt sleep. The other, more frightened part of her wanted to shake her aunt awake and make her promise she wasn't getting ill. Or growing old. Or anything else that might take her away from Kate.

Cold terror gripped her heart.

What if Ravenwood didn't want some doddering aunt wandering about his ducal estate? He hadn't even wanted Kate. He certainly wouldn't be pleased to discover he'd gained not one, but two unwanted dependents. What if he decided to execute his husbandly right to send Aunt Havens to some far off asylum and Kate never saw her again?

Dizziness assailed her. She rushed over to her aunt and pulled her into her arms. Aunt Havens was Kate's heart, her family, her lifeline. She couldn't lose her. She *wouldn't*.

"Miss Ross?" Marr, Kate's butler, stepped into the parlor. "You have a gentleman caller. Shall I show him in?"

Kate glanced up at her butler and swallowed the lump in her throat. "Show him in, please."

She placed a blanket about Aunt Havens' shoulders and sat next to her, rather than across from her. Asleep or not, they would present a united front against Ravenwood. Sort of. She took a deep breath to rally her courage.

The Duke of Ravenwood stepped into the parlor looking even more devastatingly handsome than he'd done the night before. His chestnut curls and long-lashed green eyes highlighted without softening his unsmiling lips and regal bearing.

She stood as he sketched a courtly bow, and responded with as pretty a curtsey as she could muster. She would be calm. He hadn't hoped for this turn of events any more than she had. Churlishness would help neither of them. They would have to make the best of it.

"Have you seen the scandal sheets?" she asked.

He took a seat on the chair opposite. "I don't need to."

Kate had felt the same way. For the first time in her life, she had tossed them into the fire without opening them.

Normally, she loved to read each column. To spy her name, or some unmistakable allusion to her, amongst their mindless pages.

Today was different. She pressed her lips together. The rest of her life would be different.

Ravenwood settled back in his chair. He had yet to remark upon their chaperone's gentle snores, despite the presence of needlework in her liver spotted hands.

Kate wasn't certain if his failure to acknowledge Aunt Havens made him exceptionally rude, or unexpectedly perceptive. It was not something she wished to talk about. Aunt Havens was just tired. She was going to be fine.

Ravenwood leaned forward. "Do you have a preference as to which church does the reading of the banns?"

He wanted *banns?*

She stared at him uncomprehendingly. "You're a duke. Can't you get a special license?"

"Of course. But our betrothal has been marked with enough ignominy. Banns are what most couples do. A special license is just something else for the gossips to talk about."

"We're not most couples," she said, without heat. Nothing about this was normal.

He knew that. Neither of them had wanted this. He was trying to make it easier. She tilted her head to consider him. Despite the image he projected, he wasn't an unfeeling automaton. She'd learned that last night when he'd caught her in his arms. He was trying to protect her again now.

His face was impassive. "You object to banns?"

She objected to marrying anyone. But thanks to the compromise, her wishes no longer mattered. She bit her lip. "I don't see the point to prolonging the inevitable. We have to wed. A special license is the most expedient solution. Banns won't make anyone believe we've fallen in love."

For the second time in their acquaintance, a smile twisted the Duke of Ravenwood's lips.

This time, it did not reach his eyes.

"Then there's no sense playacting." He drew a small journal from an inner coat pocket and scanned its pages. "Does one week from today fit your schedule? Ten o'clock should do. Ravenwood House has a parlor suitable for a small proceeding, if you'd rather not have the ceremony in a church."

Kate didn't have to check her calendar. She rarely scheduled anything before noon.

"Ten o'clock," she forced herself to agree. Now that she'd talked him out of banns, their impending wedding seemed all the more real. She wrapped her arms about herself. "I suppose I should bring my clothing and other personal items with me?"

He inclined his head. "You can ship ahead anything you like. I have commissioned a new armoire, expressly for your use. It is a husband's duty to provide a wedding gift for his wife."

An armoire. She fought to stay calm. She had an armoire of her own. An entire home full of things that mattered. She lifted a palm toward her papyri and painted vases. "As for the rest of my things?"

He drew back slightly. "You would wish to put these...*items* on display at Ravenwood House?"

She curled her fingers into fists. Of course her collection would not be welcome.

"You would prefer me to hold onto my townhouse and keep them here?" she returned archly.

Something shifted in his eyes. "You may keep your

townhouse, Miss Ross. It will remain yours in every way that matters."

No, it would not. She smiled through clenched teeth. Although it was not his fault, he could not deny the truth.

Nothing would be hers anymore, in any way that mattered. She had spent years building a stable life for herself by investing her modest inheritance in the four percents and her beloved museum. Now, none of that mattered.

One week from today, she would become the Duke of Ravenwood's property.

Chapter Five

Ravenwood glared at the blank page mocking him with its unblemished purity.

He was alone in his office, seated behind his father's stately escritoire. When he was a child, he would often climb up into the thick leather chair and scrawl a few lines in his journal.

During his adolescent years, particularly after the loss of his parents, those scrawled lines had ceased being a recapitulation of his day. He didn't wish to *dwell* on his grief and anger; he longed to escape it.

And so he had turned to poetry. Expressing things he *wished* would happen, rather than life as it really was. It was an escape, yes, but it also provided a brief moment of hope in days that otherwise would have none.

Days like today.

He was about to wed a woman he didn't even know. A woman who didn't know *him*—and perhaps never would.

The boy who had scribbled in his journal, the man who anguished over every dissonant couplet, that wasn't the Duke of Ravenwood. It was Lawrence Pembroke. A man with dreams and sorrows, fears and fury, apathy and abject love. 'Twas the secret side of himself he only allowed to breathe for a few moments every morning before carefully locking it away in a hidden drawer within his desk.

Today, even his recklessly romantic side had run out of hope. There was nothing left to write. The dreams inside those worn journal pages were destined to remain just that. Empty dreams.

A knock sounded upon his office door.

Ravenwood closed the stubborn journal and locked it inside its secret panel. "Come in."

Mrs. Brown, the housekeeper, cracked open the door but did not venture inside after her curtsey. "Pardon the interruption, your grace. Just wanting to see if you had any additional requirements for the wedding breakfast. There's still time to send Martha on another run to the market."

Ravenwood rubbed his face. What did he know about planning wedding breakfasts?

He'd already changed the menu twice. Even though a love match was not his fortune, he wished the breakfast to at least be tolerable to the bride.

Yet the only meal he'd ever seen Miss Ross consume was what his sister Amelia had served at her dinner party—namely, Ravenwood's favorite foods, because she'd intended to manipulate him into attending that cursed charity gala.

He would no doubt look like a perfect cad by featuring his own favorite supper dishes at a wedding breakfast, but it was the best he could do. He would not write to his bride—or worse, his sister—in search of advice. His was *not* a love match, and he refused to look like a romantical fool.

"Perhaps some canapés," he said at last. Footmen had been serving trays of them at the auction. They might be one of Miss Ross's preferred appetizers, or they might simply be the easiest thing to have on hand at her gala. In any case, at least it was another option. "That will be all."

"Yes, your grace." Mrs. Brown bobbed her respects and quickly closed the door.

Her footsteps were soundless on the carpet in the corridor, but Ravenwood had no doubt she was moving with all haste to inform Martha of her impending return to market.

Such was the power and the curse of being duke. Everyone did everything with all haste in their eagerness to accede to his commands. Had he proclaimed, *We shall serve worms in mud sauce*, such a menu would have been executed without question.

His title was not solely to blame. Being the sort of duke that he had become also had much to do with the matter.

Inheriting at a young age meant he'd had to try that much harder to live up to impossibly high expectations. To be taken seriously. To be respected.

Since then, he'd been called many things. Cold, proper, haughty, imperious, dismissive. These were not insults. They were character traits of a man who appreciated order. It was all he knew. He had perhaps grown into an outwardly hard man, but not, he felt, an unworthy one.

Until last night.

He pushed to his feet and strode from his office to an unassuming little sitting room on the opposite wing of the manor. The room was empty, save for a single gilded portrait upon the far wall. No one entered this room but Ravenwood.

No one was allowed to.

He assumed his customary position before his cherished painting and stared into its dry, cracked depths. When his uncle Blaylock had become guardian to two orphaned siblings, the man had rolled up this canvas and tossed it into a dark closet so that he could use the magnificent frame to showcase his own family.

The rescued painting contained the only family portrait of Ravenwood, his sister, and their much-loved parents.

It was an unusual piece because the artist had captured more than the family—he'd included the entire room in the background. From the vase of roses on the windowsill to the one-of-a-kind furniture before the fire, every aspect had been faithfully represented.

Ravenwood had been young at the time it had been painted, but he remembered why they'd chosen this small sitting room to star in such a portrait. The little parlor had belonged to his mother. She would invite her children into it every evening, to listen to her read aloud for an hour before the nursemaids packed them off to bed.

The duke would complain good-naturedly that listening to his wife's voice was ever so much slower than simply reading the book himself—but he never once missed an opportunity to sit in his brocade hand-carved chair before the fire, listening along with his children.

Uncle Blaylock had sold that chair, and everything else depicted in the portrait. He'd turned the cozy sitting room into a showcase for hunting trophies. Instead of housing memories of the best years of Ravenwood's childhood life, the room became a shrine to death. To loss.

The moment he reached his majority, he'd banished his uncle and the animal carcasses from Ravenwood House forever.

He hadn't been able to locate the one-of-a-kind furniture pieces the room had once boasted, nor recreate the sense of love and family it had once had. He and Amelia had been alone against the world back then.

After she'd married, it was just Ravenwood.

For another hour, anyway. He consulted his pocket watch to be certain, then sent one final gaze toward the painting.

The last people to see him as Lawrence and not the Duke of Ravenwood gazed back at him from the scarred canvas. The last people to truly know him.

All anyone saw now when they looked at him was what he allowed them to see.

He wished he could be more. He appreciated being a duke—it made him feel close to his father, who had been the most exemplary duke of *his* time—but he wished it didn't preclude him from also being a man. From having conversations deeper than "Yes, your grace" and "As you wish, your grace."

He wanted love. He wanted a family. He wanted warm nights before a crackling fire, reading aloud with his wife as they took turns cuddling their squirming children in their arms.

Not the lonely, loveless upbringing he and his sister had endured after their parents died. He wanted the warm, joyful days of love and laughter. Of family.

He didn't want a house he merely owned. He wanted a home where he *belonged*.

And yet, in an alarmingly short period of time, Ravenwood House was about to be invaded by yet another stranger. Someone else would live within these same walls, her very presence ensuring he would never be able to fully put down his guard, even in his own home. He would no longer feel comfortable.

He stalked from the sitting room toward his dressing chamber. He might not have planned to marry her, but he would not dishonor Miss Ross or his duty as a duke in any way. In half an hour, he would be ready and waiting beside the altar.

And his life would never be the same again.

Chapter Six

The Duke of Ravenwood stood in the blue parlor in the rear of his estate awaiting the arrival of his bride for the second time this year.

On the previous occasion, he had been about to marry his dead friend's paramour...until the very-much-alive brigadier returned against all odds to stop the wedding.

Ideally, Miss Ross would have no such skeletons in her past.

Edmund and his wife were seated in the front row to show their support. They were even more in love now than they'd been when Edmund had first gone off to war. When *all* of them had gone off to war. Every single one of the childhood friends that Ravenwood cared about most.

Everyone but him.

He'd felt like a failure at the time. As if he were hiding behind his title rather than putting his loyalty to the Crown first.

But managing a dukedom was no small responsibility, and Ravenwood had no heirs. If he were felled by an enemy rifle, the title would pass to none other than his Uncle Blaylock.

Ravenwood would die before he let that happen. And he'd take Uncle Blaylock down with him.

An emotional reaction to the rules of primogeniture? Absolutely. One of the few Ravenwood had ever allowed himself.

He was furious at his sister for having manipulated him into attending that ill-fated charity gala, but of course he had still invited her to the wedding. She was his sister. The only person who ever came close to knowing the true him.

As much as Ravenwood disliked time spent with most people, these past long months had been lonely without his sister.

The elder by a few years, Amelia had managed the daily minutia of Ravenwood House from the moment their parents had died. Aunt Blaylock might have *thought* she was pulling the strings, but even an adolescent Amelia had been a force of nature.

It was likely because of the Blaylocks' presence in their lives that Amelia had learned to pay close attention to every detail, to rule with cunning rather than commands.

The best thing about having a sister like Amelia was that she managed to handle everything Ravenwood hated in such a way that he didn't even need to know about it, much less deal with it. He was not required to mediate drama amongst the staff or attend public events where he would be forced into awkward conversations with people he didn't even know.

Amelia was always so good at her job that it had been easy to forget it *wasn't* her job. Until the day she'd met her husband and left Ravenwood House behind.

It had felt empty ever since.

He broke his fast alone. Lunched alone. Took tea alone. Dined alone. Sipped his port alone. And then began his day all over again.

All that, however, was about to change.

Probably.

He would not impose mealtime regulations upon a duchess. If Miss Ross wished to take her meals in the privacy of her bedchamber, he would not deny her.

No matter what he might have wished his marriage to be like.

Movement in the corridor caught his eye. He held his breath. His bride had arrived at last.

She was beautiful.

Her eyes were clear and bright. She wore a long, intricately beaded gown of pale blue silk. He had no idea if it had been commissioned for this purpose or if it was a gown she'd worn to hundreds of less-than-respectable soirées.

It didn't matter, he reminded himself. From this moment on, she was his duchess. He would treat her with the respect she deserved. She was attractive and interesting. They would get to know each other eventually. It would be fine. He would *make* their marriage succeed.

His bride's long blond hair was twisted into some sort of complicated French style, with a plethora of pearl combs holding up all but a few artful ringlets.

That was new. Her hair had been arranged much more casually the night of Amelia's dinner party, and even during the night of the charity gala. Which meant, regardless of its provenance, she was viewing their union with at least some degree of interest. Perhaps she, too, wondered what might have happened if her aunt had not interrupted them in the storage room.

Arm in arm, Mrs. Havens walked her niece all the way to the clergyman, her strut pleased as a peacock.

"Kate is going to be a duchess," she whispered to Ravenwood when they reached the altar.

"So I heard," he replied, careful not to betray his startlement at the proclamation. "I may even be the duke in question."

"I hope so. You're a handsome one." Mrs. Havens gave him a coquettish wink.

Ravenwood bowed.

Miss Ross led her aunt to the row of chairs and settled

her in the closest seat. When she resumed her place at the altar, she tossed Ravenwood a merry grin. "At least she has good taste. You *are* a handsome one."

The back of Ravenwood's neck heated, but he couldn't look away. Not when she continued to surprise him at every turn.

She didn't want to marry him. *Neither* of them wished to be in the position in which they now found themselves. They were all wrong for each other.

And yet...she looked as relaxed and comfortable as she had the night of the charity gala, when she'd stepped onstage to announce the items for auction.

Ravenwood couldn't think of anything worse than taking the stage before hundreds of people. Except perhaps being forced to marry one of them against one's will. So why was she so relaxed about the ceremony taking place? Had the allure of a dukedom trumped her disdain for the duke himself?

"You look happy," he growled, unable to keep the suspicion from his voice.

If anything, the unspoken accusation made her smile even brighter.

"Of course I'm not *happy*," she murmured, giving him a pointed gaze. "Neither are you. Yet there's nothing to be done but make the best of the situation. The fact that it's not a love match also appears to have slipped Aunt Havens' mind, so if you could bear a few smiles of your own..."

He jerked his gaze toward Mrs. Havens, who waved at him with such spontaneous delight that he could not help but smile back.

"Perfect," his bride whispered. "Thank you for playing along."

He froze. He'd actually smiled and meant it. For a brief moment, he'd forgotten his list of extremely valid concerns, and simply let himself be happy.

And it had worked.

The tightness in his chest began to lighten. Perhaps there was hope for this union after all. If they both *tried* to be happy with the other, if they both playacted convincingly enough, it might actually come true.

Hope entered his heart. What if they could coexist without clashing, starting this very night? He'd show her that doing one's duty needn't be a joyless affair. With a little luck, their marriage might succeed on a deeper level.

Perhaps someday they'd even have the large, happy family he'd always dreamed of.

Chapter Seven

Kate was fully prepared for her wedding night. She had never been kissed, but tipsy confessions from her rowdier friends had left her well aware of the mechanics of lovemaking.

At her request, they'd also gifted her a handful of "French letters"—little fitted sheaths meant to prevent the man's seed from entering the woman's body. Unfortunately, the dratted things had to soak for hours before they became soft enough to be used.

With her horror of child-birthing, however, Kate would happily wait for days, if that was how long it took the French letters to be usable. Months. Years.

Perhaps she wasn't just terrified of childbirth. Perhaps she was a tiny bit apprehensive about the creation process, as well. Who would wish to bare herself to a virtual stranger?

Even if the stranger in question was the dreadfully attractive Duke of Ravenwood. Her husband. Kate swallowed. She was now the Duchess of Ravenwood.

She didn't feel like the Duchess of Ravenwood. She felt like an outsider playacting at someone else's life. A world she knew nothing about.

Now that it was hers, however, she would do her best to

play her role. They might not have chosen each other, but now that they were married, the only path toward happiness was to move forward together.

Somehow.

Arms crossed, she leaned against the freshly constructed armoire and stared at her new bedchamber.

It was sumptuous enough for a duchess, she supposed. The furniture, the wallpaper, the carpet—everything was new and expensive and modern. A style she abhorred above all others. It had no *history*. No story to tell.

The bed was twice the size of the one she'd had at home. For obvious reasons, one might suppose, except that the chamber Ravenwood had given Aunt Havens was nearly the equal to this one in terms of size, splendor, and excess.

The doorway leading into her husband's adjoining bedchamber was of far more pressing concern.

Her lady's maid had finished preparing the scene less than an hour ago. Candles were lit, a low blaze set in the fireplace. Kate was bathed, coiffed, and dressed in the frilliest nightrail of her trousseau.

Did Ravenwood appreciate a damsel in a frilly nightrail? Kate had her doubts. But her lady's maid had insisted Ravenwood would only notice the nightrail's most important features—its breathtakingly low neckline and near-transparent material.

Lord only knew what Ravenwood would be wearing. The last man Kate had seen in a nightrail had been Great-Uncle Havens, shortly before he died of apoplexy.

It wasn't a particularly heartening image.

She tried to distract herself by planning her next project. Time would tell whether her new husband would *permit* her to continue planning events, but for now she would choose optimism. She was the one person with the passion and the connections to unite spectators of the arts with those who created it, and she would do everything in her power to make it happen.

The first step would be to rally the talent. She wouldn't be able to search for a venue until she better understood the scope of the performance. Opera singers and classic violinists would not require a large stage, but what about dancers, acrobats, choirs, and orchestras?

A knock sounded upon the adjoining door and she jumped. Heaven help her. It was time.

She stepped away from the armoire and uncrossed her arms. Perhaps it wouldn't be as bad as she feared. Perhaps she could simply continue planning in her mind whilst Ravenwood did as he pleased with her body. Her heart quickened.

No. She would never be able to ignore him. Every time he was near, she could think of nothing but him.

"Come in." Did her voice tremble? She straightened her spine. Her voice never trembled.

The adjoining door eased open with nary a creak. Orange light from the candles spilled across Ravenwood's chiseled face. She swallowed.

He was not in a nightrail. He wore buckskin breeches, a navy waistcoat, gold jacket, and a freshly pressed cravat. His chestnut curls were slightly damp, indicating he, too, had bathed moments earlier.

He looked positively delicious.

Ravenwood's eyes locked on hers. "You're dressed for bed."

"You're…not." She wasn't certain what to make of it.

He inclined his head. "I didn't want you to feel forced into physical intimacy. I am your husband, but you are my wife. Your desires matter as much as my own."

Kate gazed back at him in surprise. If he'd meant to disarm her with his thoughtful consideration, it had certainly worked. He had a right to consummation. She had expected him to execute that right and be done.

The idea that she could have a reprieve if she wished gave her the courage to welcome him in. He was giving her a chance to be comfortable with him. She would do the same.

According to her friends, plenty could happen between husband and wife prior to lovemaking.

"Come in," she repeated.

He stepped into the room and shut the door behind him.

She expected to feel closed off. Hunted. But instead she felt oddly powerful. The Duke of Ravenwood hadn't merely asked her opinion. He'd asked her *permission*. To enter a bedchamber on his own property.

He was trying to be kind. He was letting her know that as duchess, her desires *did* matter.

Now that she knew she would not be forced into con-summation without so much as a by-your-leave, what she most desired was…a kiss.

Ever since that moment in the storage shelter, she hadn't been able to quit the idea from her mind. She swallowed. Perhaps she'd been looking forward to *some* of the night's events, after all.

She lowered her gaze from his eyes to his mouth and blushed. Kissing him would be no hardship. Now that they were out of society's eye, his icy demeanor had melted to something far more intriguing.

Or perhaps she was the one who had warmed.

This was how he looked to all the other ladies. Wide shoulders, firm muscles, long eyelashes, inviting lips. They swooned at the thought of being wrapped in those strong arms. Of unleashing coiled passion. Being the one woman capable of tempting him to fan the flames.

Kate swallowed. If she were completely honest, she might even admit to having wondered on multiple occasions what kissing Ravenwood might be like. Of feeling her soft curves against his hard body. Just because she had never imagined herself in the position of ever finding out did not mean she was immune to his striking looks and quiet power.

She didn't have to suppress her attraction anymore. He

was an Adonis come to life. She had him in her bedchamber. The question was how to proceed from here, without risking childbirth.

"We were compromised over a tryst that never happened," she ventured.

He stepped closer. "Yes."

"My cousin thought you had taken liberties. Kissed me."

"All two hundred of your guests appeared to have reached the same conclusion." His tone was wry. "A bit galling, as I'd never before had a tarnished reputation."

She hesitated. "A bit galling for me as well, since to this day, I've never been kissed."

His green eyes met hers in surprise. "Never?"

"I thought you might like to…rectify matters." Her heart pounded as she waited for his reply.

With an arrogant smile, he curled a knuckle beneath her chin and angled her face toward his. "It shall be my pleasure."

Her eyes fluttered closed as he lowered his mouth to hers.

He was going to do it! Finally, they would have the kiss they'd almost shared before they were interrupted. The kiss she hadn't been able to get out of her mind. This time, there was no one to stop them.

His mouth was warm. His lips firm, but soft. She gripped his sides, unsure where or how to hold on. Each gentle brush of his lips against hers sent waves of sensation rippling across her skin.

He stroked her cheek with the pad of his thumb. She found herself responding. Kissing back. Parting her lips. Wanting more. This wasn't some untouchable, granite Adonis. This was Ravenwood. Her husband. And his kisses were as feverish as hers.

She pressed into him, eager. She wanted to taste him. To feel him. His body was hot against hers. Or perhaps *her* body was the one becoming heated.

He slid his fingers into her hair to cradle the back of her head and touched his tongue to hers.

Her pulse jumped at the wantonness. She twined her hands about his neck and rose on her toes to meet him kiss for kiss. He made her feel irresistible. Reckless. Like she could lose herself in him…and find something even better.

Her blood raced at the twin sensation of plundering and being plundered. Being known. This was *her* husband. Hers to kiss, to invite into her bedchamber.

Hers for much more.

The flimsiness of her nightrail allowed her to feel the lines of his waistcoat against her breasts. Under all those layers, did his heart beat as rapidly as hers? Could he feel the tightening of her nipples, sense the rush of excitement in her veins?

Her heart hammered. She wondered what it would be like to rub herself against him. The shameless decadence of naked breasts against a fully clothed chest. Would he rip his clothes from his body? Or would he allow her to divest him of each item, baring him inch by inch?

As if reading her thoughts, he lifted his mouth from hers just long enough to shuck his jacket and waistcoat. Before the garments even hit the floor, he pulled her back into his embrace and covered her mouth with his.

This time, there was naught but thin linen between the softness of her breasts and the hardness of his chest. She caught her breath at the sensation. He could feel her just as clearly as she could feel him. Every inch of her felt alive. Yet it wasn't enough. She craved more.

With him, she could experience anything. Everything. There would be no recriminations, no risk of scandal. So long as he wore the sheath, she could indulge her desire. They both could.

He grabbed her by the waist and trapped her between the wall and his own body, pinning her in place with his hips, his kisses.

Her head spun in heady abandon. She had watched him from afar for years. Being in his arms was more than she'd dreamed. *He* was more than she'd dreamed.

She slid her hands up the hard muscles of his arms. Had she feared the marriage bed? They were nowhere near it and she was already breathless with desire. He was so hard, so hot. She wanted to explore him. Wanted him to explore all of her. Needed him to.

Together, the rest of the world fell away. All that mattered was the two of them.

Slowly, deliberately, he slid one of his hands up from her waist to her breast. His fingertips played with her taut nipple, driving her wild with every tug, every touch.

Her kisses grew bold. Demanding. He lifted her onto the bed and covered her body with his. She reached for him. He made her feel on the edge of...*something*, and she wanted to have it all. To know pleasure. To know *him*.

He yanked up the hem of her nightrail to expose her ankles, her knees, her thighs, her—

Cool air kissed the moist heat between her legs for only a moment. Then his wicked hand took over. Cupping her, coaxing her, dipping a slick finger inside and stroking her with her own wetness. Pleasure shot through her.

She felt helpless. Powerful. Her breath grew ragged, her thoughts incoherent. He was irresistible and she wanted more. She tangled her fingers in his hair as he brought her closer and closer to a peak. He tore his mouth from hers and pinned her with his gaze.

"Do you desire me?" he rasped as he drove his finger within her. "Do you want to feel me inside you, claiming you as my own?"

"*Yes.*" It was *all* she wanted. She was nearly delirious with the wanting. Her inner muscles clenched just from the desire in his eyes as he deliberately sank his finger in deeper.

He kissed her again, then reached below to yank down

his breeches.

The thrill of anticipation raced through her. Quickly, she gestured toward the side of the bed. The sheaths would be ready. "I have a French letter soaking… over on the nightstand…"

He paused with one hand on his breeches. "A what?"

Her cheeks grew warm. "A French letter. It's a… It's a sheath for protecting—"

"I know what a French letter is." He pulled up his breeches and buttoned them back into place. "Why do you have one?"

A gasp of sudden understanding escaped her throat and she shook her head wildly to dispel his confusion. A proper young lady would have no knowledge of such devices. Any man would assume the worst: that she was a whore, or diseased.

"It's not what you think! I've never done…anything intimate before. I was just told it was easier for a man to place one of these on his member to prevent progeny than it is for a woman to deal with sponges or quinine rinses—"

He leaned back, his eyes hooded. "You're saying you don't wish to bear my children?"

The rush of familiar panic sent a wave of dizziness crashing through her. She tried to still her heart.

"I can't think of anything more horrifying than the thought of bearing *anyone's* children. It's a panic, really. Neither child nor mother has any guarantee of survival. My heart starts pounding and my vision goes black…" She took a deep, shuddering breath and forced herself to straighten her spine. Her fears no longer mattered. "I realize I don't have a choice anymore. I'm a duchess now and must do my duty. But I can't. Not yet. Eventually, I will have to do what's required, but for now I just… I wanted to be able to enjoy it. At least once."

He rose from the bed and scooped his discarded coat and waistcoat from the floor without another word.

She realized too late that his concern had been something else entirely.

"Wait," she stammered, pushing down the hem of her nightrail to cover her nakedness. "I thought you wanted…"

"Of course I want you." He paused in the open doorway connecting their bedchambers and turned inscrutable eyes toward hers. "But there are things I want more. Like a future for this dukedom. *Soon.* If you cannot promise that much, then our marriage will need to be annulled. Let us hope that does not need to happen."

He closed the door behind him. No key turned in the lock.

And yet the wall that separated them was too great for either to cross.

Chapter Eight

Ravenwood tossed his shears into the dirt and settled at the foot of his favorite cherry tree. His private garden had never felt more like home.

No matter what might be going on outside of these walls, enjoying a spot of sun beneath the shade of a comfortable tree always made him feel more at peace.

He liked being alone. He loved tending his garden. Or just letting it grow wild.

Pink geraniums and purple irises blossomed against the deep green of the grass and the brown bark of the trees. The white primula with their golden yellow centers sprang up cheerfully from their thick leaves. But his newest addition, a brightly colored smattering of dahlias, made his garden look as lush as a painting.

Happiness filled him as he gazed at all the vivid colors. He wasn't artistically inclined like Rembrandt or William Blake, and he didn't need to be in order to enjoy the art of nature. Morning dew balancing on a delicate petal brought him the same amount of joy as other men found in cockfights or shooting pheasant.

Not a particularly ducal sentiment, to be sure. England's most revered peers would never allow grass stains on their coat sleeves or muck about in the dirt like schoolchildren just to tend a flower. If they wanted a rose, they simply sent a servant with a coin to fetch one, like civilized people.

Which was why Ravenwood's walled garden was hidden beneath a cloak of ivy at the rear of his estate. And why he possessed the sole key to unlock its gate.

He would not subject the things that gave him pleasant memories—or inner peace—to the forked tongues of the *ton*. He tried not to let it bother him that no one would ever see beyond his aristocratic mask.

'Twas better for all parties that they could not.

Particularly now that his spotless reputation had taken such an ill-earned thrashing. He would need to watch his every word for the next two years to erase the damage done in a single moment.

Not that avoiding scandal was much of a challenge for a man who tended to avoid people in general.

But he wasn't alone any longer, was he? Now he had a wife. A woman he neither knew, nor understood. He tossed a blade of grass aside and pushed to his feet. That he was often happiest in solitude was not a question. Whether he could be happy with her, or she with him…

No future family? He would not resign himself or his dukedom to such a fate. But while begetting an heir was both a must and a priority, the thought of forcing himself upon a wife who lay there in terror simply because it was her duty did not paint a pretty picture.

Annulling their marriage, however, was not a step Ravenwood would ever take lightly.

Not only would she be ruined in the process, he took his wedding vows as seriously as he took his loyalty to the Crown. *For better or for worse* meant not giving up at the first sign of adversity.

He would simply treat her as he treated the rest of the *beau monde*. He would be polite, play his assigned role, and wear the mask that she wanted—or at least expected—to see.

For now.

To his surprise—and pleasure—the passion they had shared had been as fast and as hot as quicksilver. There was no denying their attraction. In the space of a breath, their simple kiss had led to him shedding clothing and tumbling them both into bed.

That was more than promising. All she needed was time to get to know him. Perhaps that was what they both needed. To come together as a couple, rather than as strangers.

He was convinced their union could work. He just had to convince his wife.

Mind set, he quit the garden sooner than he had planned. It would survive without him. His relationship, on the other hand, would not.

Ravenwood went straight to his chamber to wash up and change into fresh clothes. It had been *his* bedchamber for over a decade, and had never once struck him as particularly cold or lonely. Until last night.

Sleep had not come easily. He had stared at his tester until the wee hours, wondering if his wife was doing the same thing. Now that he was back from his garden, perhaps they would have a chance to speak.

When he emerged from his dressing chamber and enquired as to her whereabouts, he learned she was taking tea in the yellow parlor with her aunt.

Ravenwood nodded to himself. Perfect. Not only would the presence of a third party make conversation less awkward, at last he would also learn what his wife liked to eat besides fish and canapés.

Today, they would stop being strangers. Very soon, they would truly be husband and wife.

Both ladies were holding saucers of tea when he entered the parlor. He bowed to them both, and motioned for them to remain seated and enjoy their tea.

"Good afternoon, your grace. Mrs. Havens. I trust you

slept well?"

Laugh lines radiated from the corners of Mrs. Havens' eyes as she grinned up at him. "Like a babe. I would've found a duke to marry myself if I'd had any idea how soundly I'd be able to sleep."

He blinked. "I am pleased the accommodations meet your approval. And you, madam?" He turned to his wife. "Do you lack for anything?"

She squinted at him for a moment, then burst out laughing.

At first he stiffened, assuming her mirth to be mockery. But then she shook her head.

"Please don't tell me I'm to spend the rest of my life being referred to as 'Madam' and 'Your grace' by my own husband. My name is Katherine. If you feel comfortable doing so, you have my leave to use it."

Mrs. Havens raised a finger at her niece. "Some people might appreciate being able to command such elevated honorifics."

"Yes, yes." She waved a dismissive hand. "I'll be certain to require such acknowledgements when I find myself amongst mere earls and viscounts. But there's no need for stiff formality in one's own home, is there?"

Ravenwood remained silent. His father had never referred to his mother with anything less than the full respect her position deserved, and Ravenwood had always intended to follow that example.

However, his goal was to encourage his wife to think warmly of him. To welcome him into her heart and her bed. If that meant calling her "Katherine", then so it would be.

He began by taking a seat across from the ladies and accepting a cup of tea.

Mrs. Havens leaned forward. "Kate was just relating the most diverting story about the time she belted out a sailor's rhyme in an empty theatre, only to realize dozens of people on the other side of the curtain had heard the whole thing."

Katherine turned pink with laughter. "I daresay I was more careful after that. I don't even let myself attend musicales anymore."

Ravenwood blinked. At moments like these, he was glad to wear a mask of stone. Her anecdote wasn't humorous. It was mortifying. Had such an embarrassment happened to him, he would never have repeated the tale.

And yet.

He had always equated Miss Katherine Ross with "flighty, irresponsible hoyden." He was perhaps mistaken in the first two pronouncements. Her antiquities museum and her production of the charity gala were proof of her business acumen and philanthropic spirit.

But hoyden? Absolutely. She didn't take anything in life seriously, least of all herself. Her associations with those of questionable reputation had been proof of that.

Ravenwood frowned. He couldn't imagine what it might be like to not care a button what anyone else thought.

The idea was both fascinating and appalling. He cared tremendously what other people thought. His peers. The Crown. Society at large. Interpreting social cues was not always easy for him, which was why he relied on rules. They saved him.

Proper social mores were the best way for all parties to know how to comport themselves. When everyone agreed on what constituted suitable decorum, no one was left guessing. Acceptable behavior was both expected, and easily achievable.

For people who didn't belt out sailor ditties in empty theatres.

Mrs. Havens set down her cup and saucer and rose to her feet with a knowing smile. "When couples are this quiet, it's usually because there is too much to say. I've plenty of embroidery to get back to. Kate, you know where to find me. Have a lovely tea."

In dismay, Ravenwood watched Mrs. Havens quit the

parlor. Her presence had meant he and his new wife wouldn't need to broach the previous night's failings. Not yet. Not until circumstances changed enough to warrant renewed discussion.

Which left what? He didn't know Katherine well enough to start a conversation she'd be passionate about.

He cleared his throat. "What were you doing on stage in the first place?"

Her smile lit her entire face. "My friends and I had been considering a plan to unite the stratified circles of art."

"To what?" This time, he didn't have to try to keep his face blank. He had absolutely no idea what she was talking about.

She touched her chin. "Would you say that London is home to a boast-worthy population of world-class artists, musicians, dancers, and the like? More than just the most famous faces we typically see on the stage?"

"Yes, of course." He stared at her over steepled fingers and wondered where the topic was headed.

He held the best private box in the Royal Theatre and considered himself something of an aficionado, but he had never put more thought to the experience than simply enjoying the play.

Katherine's words came faster. "Would you also agree that London is home to a rich population of art and music aficionados, who would attend such programs twenty-four hours a day, if such a feat were possible? Particularly during the Season?"

"I suppose so," he answered hesitantly, no doubt in his mind that he was stepping into a trap.

She leaned forward. "I intend to join the two groups. London is home to countless talented individuals who lack the funds to purchase paints or instruments or ballet lessons. And there is certainly no shortage of wealthy aristocrats who could easily afford to sponsor such individuals, thereby becoming true patrons of the arts."

"You plan to ask your peers to donate money to un-trained artists?" he asked doubtfully.

"I plan to *prove* what a good investment it is." Her blue eyes shone. "I intend to found a monthly gala, in which undiscovered visual and performing artists of all types can take their turn on the stage. The audience will be full of future investors—and spectators who simply wish to enjoy an evening's entertainment."

He frowned. "And then what?"

"After each performance, there will be an opportunity to mingle. Music lovers will discover budding musicians to sponsor, and so on. Most importantly, both groups will be interacting. Artists not only deserve respect—they need money to live, and to work on their craft. If peers want to keep enjoying the arts, we need to ensure the performers can thrive."

He shook his head. Yes, peers did wish to keep enjoying the arts. No, he did not think performers should achieve the same level of respect.

He didn't hide his skepticism. "You think Lady Jersey will begin handing out Almack's vouchers to actresses?"

"Oh, obviously not." She shrugged. "Actors and musicians will likely never enjoy a truly elevated social status. But nor should they be seen as inferior creatures."

"They *are* inferior," he pointed out dryly.

"Surely we can agree that they shouldn't be seen as *unworthy* creatures at least," she said, eyes flashing. "Not by me and not by you. I hope my husband is the first in line to give a sponsorship to some deserving artist."

His smile was tight. "Just as my presence was so beneficial the night of the charity auction?"

"Unintended consequences occurred," she conceded. "But yes—your presence attracted a greater number of attendees, and therefore raised a greater amount of funds for Daphne's charity work. This is the same idea. I don't see—"

"I'll be first to donate," he forced himself to say despite

his misgivings. He had come here not to argue, but to woo. A happy wife would *want* to bear her husband's children. He cleared his throat. "I'll also be last to donate, and give a stipend to every participant who fails to attract a proper sponsor of his own."

"Truly?" She stared at him in wonder. "You would donate so much?"

He lifted a palm. 'Twas just money. He doubted all of the artistic hopefuls would later become front stage sensations, but there was no reason not to give them the chance to try. If he had been born not a duke but a penniless poet, a society like the one Katherine proposed would be a life-changing opportunity.

The difficult part would be surviving the event itself. He had always enjoyed his private theatre box because it was just that: private.

Being expected to make conversation with hundreds of people sounded like hell on earth.

His discomfort with being on display was one of the primary reasons he was rarely seen at society events. The last few balls he'd attended had either been at the request of his sister or one of his childhood friends. Nothing else would tempt him to subject himself to the public eye and crowded spaces.

Except, apparently, a wife.

He rolled back his shoulders. Not only was he a man who knew his duty as a husband, he sought more than an ordinary marriage. He wanted friendship. A house that felt like a home.

If his monetary contribution and physical presence would make his wife happy, then it was what he must do. Who knew where her experiment might lead? She believed so firmly and so completely in herself and her ideals... Perhaps she would start to feel the same about him, too.

"Of course I will support you," he said. "It will be my pleasure."

"There's something else I'd like to ask you. Perhaps if we…" she trailed off and bit her lip.

He leaned forward. "Yes?"

Before she could respond, Simmons, the head butler, appeared in the doorway. "Pardon the interruption, your grace. The coach is ready."

Ravenwood's muscles tightened. Parliament. Splendid. Preparing himself for long hours sequestered with so many people was almost physically painful.

He was always expected to know things, to speak eloquently, to be capable of persuading the masses… It was enough to shrink his stomach into a cramped ball of dread.

He schooled his features into a blank mask. He knew what was expected of him. And he had to leave now, or risk being late.

He pushed to his feet and bowed to his wife. "We'll talk another time."

As much as he wished to learn about Katherine's other idea, it would have to wait. Duty always came first.

"Of course," she said without meeting his eyes. "There will be plenty of chances for tea."

Something in her voice, however, indicated there might not.

Chapter Nine

The following morning, Kate was thrilled to learn that Ravenwood House was expecting guests for the noon meal. She hadn't seen her husband since he'd left for Parliament, and was grateful for an opportunity to spend more time together.

Since they'd last spoken, she had realized that the last thing she wanted was an annulment. Not because she would lose her reputation—an avowed spinster like her was certainly strong enough to handle that.

What she didn't want to lose was Ravenwood.

He surprised her at every turn. He had accepted Aunt Havens. And the passion between them…

A flush rose to her cheeks. If they would have consummated their marriage on their wedding night, she suspected she would have enjoyed it very much. She hadn't been able to stop thinking about his kisses, his touch. What might have happened next, if the moment hadn't been ruined.

If anything, the worst part about making love would have been letting him go when he decided to return to his own chamber.

Bearing a child, however… She tried to swallow her panic.

If she refused to try, he would be within his rights to

request an annulment. Yet how was she supposed to bear an heir? No matter how much she craved intimacy with her husband, her passion vanished at the memories of all the mothers whose children had not survived.

She shuddered. Best to worry about that later.

Right now, the most important things were extending an olive branch to her husband—and being a good hostess to their luncheon guests.

Hope and anticipation lightened her spirits. One of the things she had treasured most about her townhouse was its constant influx of friends and acquaintances of all walks of life.

The only pastime even more cherished than catching up with old friends was meeting new ones. She had never met the Blaylocks, but they were apparently cousins of some sort. Ravenwood's sister, Lady Amelia, would be joining them just for the occasion.

Kate found a sitting room with a picturesque view of the front garden and perched at the bay window to wait.

Aunt Havens preferred to settle in one of several wing-back chairs in order to pass the time with her embroidery. Kate had never had the patience for such slow, careful work, but normally adored watching her aunt's inventive designs blossom to life.

At the moment, however, she was far more intrigued by the coach wending its way up the primary Ravenwood House entrance. An older woman was handed out first, followed by young lady obviously with child, and similarly-aged young man with bright red hair.

Kate clasped her hands together in delight. Whoever these cousins were, they were already fascinating.

Someone as high in the instep as her husband would undoubtedly hew to the belief that women who "increasing" should remain shuttered in their homes and well out of sight from Polite Society.

That this family obviously did not—and intended to call

upon Ravenwood without the slightest concern for the "rules"—meant this would be a very interesting luncheon indeed.

A frown creased her brow. Perhaps she had underestimated her new husband. It was entirely possible that his haughty air was reserved for public occasions and that, amongst family, he was more relaxed.

She doubted Ravenwood would ever go so far as to become *boisterous*, but he had surprised her on several occasions thus far, and she would be quite pleased if he did so again. He wasn't just some buck whose kisses set her world afire. To her pleasant surprise, she quite *liked* him.

Ravenwood's relentless self-control might make him a bore at parties, but his strong work ethic and prioritization of duty were qualities one could not help but admire. He was an excellent duke and a great asset to the House of Lords. And he had thus far been an exceptionally understanding husband.

If their home life were considerably more relaxed, their joyless union might become more than enjoyable. She had missed him while he was at Parliament. She would make him miss her, too. They could have a happy marriage, she was certain. It would just take time.

She would be the best possible wife. And an exemplary duchess. Starting with making friends with the first guests to pay their respects.

Excitedly, Kate looped her arm through her aunt's and headed to the front parlor to meet her new cousins. The redheaded man's face brightened the moment she and her aunt entered the room.

"Your grace!" he exclaimed. "I see my cousin is not yet present to perform the introductions, so I will simply have to do them myself. I'm Quentin Blaylock. These lovely women are my wife and my mother, both conveniently sharing the name Mrs. Blaylock." He laughed, as did his wife.

His mother did not.

"Pleased to meet you, your grace," said the younger Mrs. Blaylock, smiling widely. "Pardon me if I don't curtsey—I'm afraid if I attempt the maneuver, I'll tumble over and have the baby right here."

A laugh startled out of Kate's throat at the incongruous comment. The Blaylocks were delightfully vulgar and oddly charming, all at the same time. She could scarcely believe them related to Ravenwood at all.

"The pleasure is mine, I assure you. This is my great-aunt, Mrs. Havens. And as you've already surmised, I'm…" She hesitated.

On the one hand, it felt queer to be constantly referred to as *Her Grace* instead of by her name. On the other hand, this was Ravenwood's house and Ravenwood's family, and perhaps she ought not be too quick to dispense with formalities without her husband here to guide her.

"I'm the new duchess," she said instead. "I'm afraid I am still getting used to the role."

"What's to get used to? I'm sure my cousin takes care of absolutely everything," Mr. Blaylock said teasingly, then shot a pointed look at his mother. "That's Papa's doing, you know. Always saying *you'd make a horrid duke* and *you'll never live up to your father—*"

"Old history," the elder Mrs. Blaylock hissed. "And not something that should be discussed with the new duchess."

He rolled his eyes good-naturedly. "She ought to know who she's speaking with, don't you think?" He leaned toward Kate and lowered his voice. "I'm second in line for the title, third once you do your duty. We live in Shropshire. It's a small country cottage, but you're welcome anytime. Ravenwood's like a brother to me. A distant one. It's my father he can't stand. Can't say I blame him. Whenever Father has too much drink, he likes to remind the room at large that he's one bad shellfish away from becoming duke."

Kate clapped her hands to her mouth in horror. Poor Ravenwood!

"No, no, we're used to him spouting off," Mr. Blaylock assured her. "It's just his way. That's why Father hasn't been allowed on this property since the moment Ravenwood reached his majority. Where *is* the blighter, by the way? Never say he's too busy with paperwork to share a meal with his family."

"I..." She shot a desperate glance at Aunt Havens, then nearly sagged in relief when a familiar brunette walked in the front door.

"Cousin!" Lady Amelia handed her pelisse to a footman, then bussed cheeks with the Blaylock family. "I have just informed the groundskeeper that yes, you may do a spot of fowling after luncheon."

The younger Mrs. Blaylock's mouth fell open. "How did you—"

"Lady Amelia knows everything," Mr. Blaylock interrupted with a laugh. "She probably sensed a weight difference upon our carriage axles and deduced the presence of a sporting gun on board for flushing partridge. How do you do, cousin? Isn't married life grand?"

"It is indeed," Lady Amelia agreed. "You must be starving. If you'll follow me to the dining room, lunch will be served shortly. And never you fear—neither fish nor strawberries shall be present at the table."

Kate's face heated as her stomach twisted. Lady Amelia was no longer mistress of this house, yet *she* had ordered the staff. *She* had chosen the menu. *She* had known what should be served and not served, and at precisely what time.

Meanwhile, Kate had spent the morning peering out a picture window like an insipid child awaiting Father Christmas. Just because she'd been looking forward to seeing her husband and meeting new people.

Kate swallowed. The moment the Blaylocks left, she would dedicate herself to learning everything she could about running the estate.

Her throat went dry. The prospect suddenly seemed overwhelming.

She took her place across from her husband at the table. Or would have, were he present. He had not left the grounds—her morning vigil by the front window ensured she would have noticed a departure—and he, too, must be suffering hunger pangs by now.

Which could only mean he was avoiding the party on purpose. She hesitated. Were his cousins too "common" for his taste?

She frowned. Despite the Blaylocks' country vulgarity, they were family. Ravenwood's conspicuous absence dishonored himself as much as it did his cousins.

Not that she should have expected otherwise. He rarely presented himself in society as anything less than a holier-than-thou sovereign, and was operating precisely as advertised. She bit her lip.

Now that she was his duchess, would he expect her to follow his example and eschew contact with individuals of lesser status?

Her stomach tightened. If he was too good for his own cousins, he no doubt despised her associations with musicians, artists, and those who aspired to be such. In avoiding the lower classes, he was missing out on getting to know the largest percentage of the country he loved so much.

Well, Kate would not adhere to such an edict. Instead, she would do as Lady Amelia did, and treat the Blaylocks—and all people—with empathy, respect, and unflagging politeness.

Aunt Havens, who had spent decades married to a parson, conversed freely with all parties at the table without batting a single eyelash. As a midwife for most of those years, Aunt Havens had seen everyone in Maidstone at their best and their worst, and treated them all the same.

That was the example Kate had grown up with, and the one she intended to follow.

It might not be a duchessy attitude, but it was the only course Kate could take and still live with herself.

She threw herself into the conversation as if it were one of the many dinner parties she'd hosted at her townhouse over the years. She told amusing anecdotes, inquired into each Blaylock's individual hobbies and aspirations, and listened with a genuine smile on her face to let them know how pleased she would be if they continued to stop by for visits.

After they quit the dining room for a promenade out-of-doors, however, she quietly asked the butler whether her husband was indeed hard at work in his office.

"No, your grace," Simmons answered, his eyes thoughtful. "His grace has spent the past few hours in his garden."

In his *garden?* Kate was so nonplused by this explanation that the butler returned to his post before she could think of anything else to say. She turned around to discover Lady Amelia watching her in silence.

Kate raised her chin. "Am I missing something? Something else, I mean?"

"I'm afraid you might be," Lady Amelia said softly. "Ravenwood's garden is his private sanctuary. Only he has the key."

"Ravenwood...has a secret garden?" Kate repeated uncomprehendingly. "Why is he there instead of here?" She shook her head. "I suppose a duke can do as he pleases."

"Not often." Lady Amelia's expression was gentle. "My brother doesn't just feel uncomfortable around his cousins. He feels uncomfortable around *people*. All people."

Kate stared at her. Ravenwood? Uncomfortable around people?

"He hates the attention," Lady Amelia explained. "Of being expected to say or do the right thing in all circumstances. And yet, as duke, it is his duty to stand out in

Parliament, mingle in society, and converse at dinner parties. He forces himself to do so for as long as he can, but occasionally it becomes too much, even for him, and he seeks a moment of peace alone in his garden. He'll make himself known before our cousins leave. Ravenwood would never shirk his duty entirely."

Kate's eyes widened in belated understanding. Ravenwood didn't hate commoners any more than peers. He hated being forced to interact with *people*. All of them.

"Getting him to attend the charity auction took every wile at my disposal," Lady Amelia confessed. "I doubt even I will be able to convince him to attend another public event for a very long time."

Kate's cheeks heated as she compared her quick judgment of Ravenwood's absence today with the conversation they had shared the day before. She had demanded his presence at her upcoming event without a single thought to how he might feel about attending. She had assumed any disinterest would be due to the inferiority of the persons involved, and dismissed any reluctance as ducal hauteur.

In reality, she had invited him to attend his worst nightmare.

Not just attend… Sit in the front row. Speak with his peers. Sponsor the performers. Make a public spectacle of himself.

And he had said yes. For her.

Her breath caught.

She followed Lady Amelia to the door, but hesitated before joining the others for a promenade.

The only thought in her head was Ravenwood. She wished she could go to him. Thank him. Tell him he needn't worry about entertaining guests in the future. She wouldn't put him through it. If he needed his space, she would give it to him.

Even if it meant being lonely, herself.

"Your grace?" The butler's voice was low, his eyes

kind. "The staff is on standing orders to answer every question you might pose of us and to grant every request. If you like, I shall have a footman escort you to his grace's private garden immediately."

Kate shook her head, throat tight. "No, thank you. When he wishes me to know where it is, he will invite me himself."

Chapter Ten

From that moment forward, Kate spent every waking moment learning everything she could about managing the Ravenwood household. These were the skills her husband valued. By mastering them, he would come to value her, too.

There was just so much to learn. The estate was twenty times as large as her little townhouse had been. The grounds, even larger.

A sleepless week flashed by. There were so many servants, so many rules, so many ways for things to go wrong. But she could do it. She had to. This was her life now. And the most obvious way to impress her husband.

Kate rubbed her face. She would prove herself a worthy duchess if it killed her. She smiled grimly. It might.

She had barely slept these past several days. due to long hours of interviewing the staff and everyone they interacted with. She did her best to learn and memorize everything she could. Ravenwood was worth it.

He deserved a wife he could be proud of. Kate wanted to *be* someone he could be proud of. She wanted to be important. Not to the estate, but to him. She wanted to be missed.

Even half as much as she missed him.

The running of Ravenwood House was a great deal of work. Learning the inner workings was even harder. Kate didn't mind work—in fact, she thrived on it, which was one of the main reasons she'd started her museum—but this was different.

Ravenwood House was supposed to be her new home. Yet she awoke each morning with the sensation of living in someone else's house. She rubbed her forehead and stared at her piles of notes.

While he spent his days in his office and his nights at Parliament, she'd begun journals. She kept records of staff, schedules, duties, and restrictions, much the same way she kept detailed notes of every object's history and provenance in her antiquities museum. The thought made her miss her old treasures all the more.

This *was* someone else's house. Ravenwood's, to be precise, even though he was rarely here. But their home was meant to be Kate's as well. She shouldn't have to feel so out-of-place and lonely.

There must be something that could be done.

Ravenwood had his secret garden. Thus, there was no reason why she could not have a small corner of this enormous manor to call her own. A few antiquities. A cozy hearth. One tiny room in all this vastness where she could finally feel like she belonged.

Ever since the butler's pronouncement that the staff had been explicitly ordered to grant any request she might have, Kate had been unable to quit the idea from her head.

She wouldn't nuisance Ravenwood with such an insignificant request. He was responsible for some sort of parliamentary committee that was swallowing every spare moment of his time. The greatest favor she could do for him was to suss out an appropriately unassuming little room as far from his office as possible, so as not to bother him when he *was* at home.

It took days to walk every inch of the estate, evaluating

each potential chamber in her spare time. At last, she found the perfect parlor in the rear of the property. It was the smallest, emptiest, most out-of-the-way room in the manor, making it uniquely perfect as a space to call her own.

She clasped her hands together and twirled about the little gold-and-white room with a smile. She'd settled on Egyptian, just like the sitting room in her old townhouse. In fact, she had sent for every object in that very room. The crates would be arriving at any moment. She grinned.

If she couldn't go home, she would simply make a new home right here.

The only item in the otherwise vacant parlor was a family portrait upon the far wall. She gazed at the family in the portrait. 'Twas not difficult to pick out the previous Duke of Ravenwood. He looked almost exactly like her husband.

A man who confounded her expectations at every turn.

The portrait looked less than twenty years old. Normally, Kate was fanatical about historical accuracy when she themed a chamber, but in this case, she intended to leave the painting exactly where it hung. It would be the centerpiece, the key difference between her previous Egyptian sitting room and this new one.

The old townhouse had belonged to Kate. This new home, she shared with her husband. She *liked* feeling that he would be a part of her special room as well.

He was exactly what she'd always believed him to be. Proud. Arrogant. Intelligent. But he was also so much more than that. So much deeper. She hadn't imagined him to possess many secrets, much less something so romantic as a private garden.

If she'd begun to like him before, she was positively fascinated by him now. She just wished there was more opportunity to spend time together. Learning about his estate did make her feel closer to him, but it was no substitute for the man himself.

Until recently, she had believed life was always easy for a duke. She now realized his had been no easier than her own. They had both lost their parents at a young age. But where Kate had been taken in by the most kindhearted, loving people she could ever imagine being blessed with, Ravenwood had spent his formative years desperately proving himself better than the uncle who wished him dead in order to inherit.

He'd overcome that, obviously. In spades. He'd also mastered his own shyness to such a degree that Kate hadn't even suspected he possessed the trait. Much as she never would have imagined him toiling in a garden.

He was the most unpredictable man she had ever known. A puzzle for her to unwrap and put together. Her heart thumped at the idea.

She had never felt awkward amongst groups of people, large or small, but anxiousness now plagued her when she thought of her husband. What must he think of her? She did not know. Wasn't certain she wished to know.

Did he even wish to spend more time with her? Or was she simply one more name in the long list of people he'd feel more comfortable without?

She stared down at her journals and their pages of notes. Her fingers trembled. She would not be doing all of this if some part of her hadn't decided to avoid an annulment at all costs. Now that she had Ravenwood, she didn't want to let go.

She had hundreds of friends, thousands of acquaintances, but the only opinion that truly mattered, the only person whose respect she most desired…was his.

Perhaps once she proved herself Lady Amelia's equal in the management of this estate, he would *want* her as his wife, rather than simply be shackled to her. Perhaps someday, they could be partners. She bit her lip.

They still had not consummated their marriage. He hadn't so much as knocked upon her bedchamber, much less kissed her, since that night. A week was perhaps not a terribly long time, but to a bride who spent every night staring at their adjoining door, it had felt like a lifetime.

She knew she had disappointed him. Their compromise had ruined his life as much as it had ruined hers. But it didn't have to be terrible indefinitely. She was learning the estate. Starting to feel at home. She took a deep breath. Soon, she would make him proud.

Footsteps sounded in the hall. "Your grace? Where would you like these crates?"

Joy filled her at the sight of her carefully wrapped treasures. "Set them against that wall until we can retrieve what's inside. Have you a hammer? Yes, perfect. Go ahead and open the lids. That's one of the pharaoh's chairs! They'll go over there, please. Be on the lookout for carvings. You found the crate of scarab vases? Wait for the lion's paw tables first. Those will go over here. Oh, the papyri! Please mount them on the walls opposite the windows."

The footmen rushed to do her bidding. Every corner of the room would soon have history to feast her eyes upon.

She bounced on her toes. This many people, this many moving parts, was absolutely invigorating. Excitement coursed through her. She loved decorating, loved history, loved rediscovering ancient treasures. This parlor wouldn't be a mirror image of her old sitting room—it would be even better.

"Kate? Kate?" Aunt Havens dashed into the room, eyes wide. Her voice was high pitched and desperate. "I can't find the dog!"

The footmen froze in unison, their brows furrowing with confusion.

Kate ignored them and forced herself to smile. "Don't be concerned, Aunt. You know how he likes to hide under beds. This house is a positive treasure trove of new hiding spots for him. He's perfectly fine."

Relief washed across Aunt Havens' face. "You're right. Of course you're right. I'm being foolish."

Kate gave her a heartfelt embrace. She held onto her aunt a moment too long. "Where's your embroidery? If you work on that for a while, I'm sure he'll turn up. You know how he hates to be ignored."

Aunt Havens chortled. "True, true. I will do exactly that. Thank you, my dear."

Kate kept the merriest smile she could firmly in place until her aunt disappeared down the corridor.

It was a bad day, that's all. Everyone was entitled to one now and again.

The move hadn't been any less stressful on Aunt Havens, so it was little wonder she should have a momentary relapse.

Weeks had passed since she'd last mentioned the dog. Months, perhaps. Kate straightened her spine. Aunt Havens was getting better, not worse.

In a few hours, she would be the same wise old aunt again, and have no memory at all of even asking such a silly thing. There was positively no cause for alarm. Aunt Havens was fine. She was going to outlive them all.

"There's no dog," she said to the staring footmen, her voice coming out harsher than she intended. "Are you finished unpacking the crates?"

They still didn't move. The noise had attracted more than Aunt Havens.

"What's going on in here?" asked a low, dangerous voice.

Kate whirled to see her husband towering in the parlor entryway. Her stomach dropped at the sight.

Veins stood out on his face and neck. His eyes were wild. "What are you doing in here? Get out. Get everything out. *Now!*"

Fear and confusion gripped her. She reached out a hand. "I—"

"Do not speak to me until this room is precisely how you found it. And then never enter it again."

His words were a snarl, but his eyes bespoke some unfathomable hurt. Before she could explain her actions, he turned and stalked away.

Chapter Eleven

No matter how badly Kate longed for an explanation, she refused to gossip about her husband to their servants. He wanted a proper duchess. She was trying her best to be the sort of wife he might have actually chosen.

It meant keeping quiet. It meant staying out of his way. Above all, it meant keeping her personality as bottled up as possible.

She yearned for their marriage to succeed, and yet kept managing to push Ravenwood further away, without even knowing why. Every time she risked being herself, it only made things worse.

As soon as her cherished possessions had been stuffed back into crates and summarily returned to Kate's townhouse, she paid a visit to the one person who might have answers.

Lady Amelia.

"Did you ask him about it?" was the first thing Lady Amelia said after pouring a fresh cup of tea.

Kate shook her head. The moment had been too awful. She hadn't seen him since. Her heart twisted. "If you could have seen his face... No. It was not the moment for questions."

Lady Amelia nodded as if that was what she'd expected

to hear. "I imagine not. It's…complicated."

Kate waited. She was not hungry for tea. She wanted to understand her husband. To make him happy.

"You have a fine eye for decorating," Lady Amelia said presently. "How would you describe the interior style of Ravenwood House?"

Dreary was the first word to come to Kate's mind. She opted not to share it.

"Staid. Classic," she said instead. "I imagine it looks much the same now as it did twenty or thirty years ago when your father was duke."

"It looks *exactly* the same." Lady Amelia sighed. "Down to the button. Every carpet, every nightstand, every sconce upon every wall. It is like walking into the past."

"Your brother kept it that way as a shrine to your parents?"

Lady Amelia's smile was mirthless. "If only it were that simple. Uncle Blaylock—the one you did *not* meet the other day, and likely never will—was our guardian after our parents died. He was merely heir presumptive, but he acted as though the dukedom already belonged to him. His first act was to remake Ravenwood House into his own."

"He…redecorated?"

"He gutted our home," Lady Amelia said flatly. "Uncle Blaylock fancies himself the world's greatest hunter. Down came cherished heirlooms and Mother's collection of watercolors. Up went Uncle Blaylock's trophies. The room you described was once our favorite room in the entire estate. Father had commissioned custom-carved furniture as a special gift to the family, so we would have somewhere to read together. Uncle Blaylock sold every piece in order to put boar's heads upon the walls, bear carcasses upon the floor, and fill the shelves with stuffed chipmunks with marble eyes that Uncle Blaylock stitched himself."

Kate shivered. "It's empty now, the parlor. Save for a single portrait upon the wall."

Lady Amelia nodded. "That portrait was painted in that very room, and is the sole extant memory of how the parlor used to look. The missing pieces were sold, or broken, or lost. There's no chance of ever having them back again. Of recreating the room that housed our happiest childhood memories. Ravenwood has spent the past many years restoring the rest of the manor to the exact condition it was when our parents were still alive, but the thing he wants the most is the one thing he cannot have."

"To restore your family's sitting room."

"To be *happy*. He thinks the only way to create happiness in the future is by resurrecting the past. It doesn't work. I tried it. The only way to be happy in the future, is to be happy *now*."

"How?" Kate asked dully. Her stomach sank. Their problems weren't as simple as her having a horror of childbirth and him needing an heir. He didn't want just any family. He wanted the one he used to have. He wanted to rewrite time. "For better or worse, he's stuck with me."

"For better or worse," Lady Amelia agreed and took a sip of tea. "When I set out to get a husband, Lord Sheffield was the furthest candidate from my mind. Just because you didn't plan to end up with each other doesn't mean you're wrong for each other."

Kate smiled as if this advice had bolstered her spirits, and thanked Lady Amelia for her time.

After she climbed back into the coach, she stared blankly out of the side window for a long moment before remembering to give the driver directions for the next stop.

When she had set out that afternoon, her initial idea had been to start visiting artists and performers in order to develop interest in participating in her upcoming patronage event. Her passion for the arts was the one thing capable of keeping her mind off her husband, or what they were going to do about their marriage.

And yet, she was no longer thinking about opera singers

or classical violinists, but rather how she might do the impossible and bring Ravenwood's empty room back to life.

Perhaps if she could do the impossible, the one thing even he had been unable to achieve, he would finally realize how much she yearned to please him.

She realized she was not part of his past. That she might never matter half as much to him as the portrait hanging in the empty parlor.

But if she could give him back his memories, perhaps he would no longer need to long for the past. Perhaps then they could work together toward their future.

Her theatre connections that society so disparaged meant that Kate personally knew a set designer so talented, she had no doubt he would be able to recreate furniture from a painting.

The problem was the painting itself.

She had been forbidden from entering the sitting room. Allowing Mr. Devonshire to use the parlor as his workroom while he carved each piece was likewise not a possibility.

Besides, she suspected such an unusual gift would be much better received as a surprise. If she asked Ravenwood outright, he might say no. That recreation was not the same as restoration. That if his mother had never sat on that precise chair, it simply wasn't good enough.

Just like Kate wasn't good enough.

As soon as they arrived back home, she trudged back up to her escritoire and resumed studying the journals. Tomorrow, she would take a break for a moment. Play a game with her aunt.

Tonight, she would concentrate on Ravenwood.

Chapter Twelve

Ravenwood stalked the corridors of his estate in a temper.

From the moment he'd realized he was going to have to wed a stranger, his life had been destined to change. He understood that. He accepted it.

What he hadn't fully comprehended was the scope and severity of said change. Or the possibility that he would lose not only the inherent freedom of bachelorhood, but his grasp on all the things he held most dear.

Like his right to peace in his own household. The sanctity of the happy memories he cherished in his past. Or the possibility of building a peaceful, predictable future.

Laughter spilled from an open doorway down the hall. His wife was undoubtedly playing whist with her aunt again. And trading betting fish. His lips pinched together at the impropriety.

Katherine was chaos. Ravenwood preferred order.

He had also been rather partial to the idea of a loving, doting wife. Someone who would *wish* to spend her evenings with him. And her nights. Someone he felt happier with than without.

He'd tried to be understanding of Katherine's viewpoint. To give her the space and freedom to get to know Ravenwood House. To get to know *him*. Perhaps even to miss him.

He'd also begun to know her.

Whilst he might yearn for a family of his own, she had no need for such fantasies. She'd brought her family with her. What did she want with a baby, when her aunt was often a child herself?

Katherine's life had already been full, long before she'd married Ravenwood. She collected friends the way some people collected gloves. Juggled more cultural projects in one year than most people attended in a lifetime.

She wasn't looking for an "other half." She had an excess of followers. And a hectic schedule. Her life and heart were more than full. There was no need—or room— for Ravenwood.

These were facts. Some men might accept them. But Ravenwood hated feeling superfluous in his own home. It ought to be a haven. *His* haven.

He strode into the yellow parlor intending to command Katherine to cease being so disruptive. There was work to be done. They had an image to uphold.

He hadn't expected to catch her trying to teach his butler to dance.

"Ravenwood!" she exclaimed, her eyes sparkling. "Splendid. Aunt Havens is finding it difficult to waltz by her lonesome. Be her partner, won't you? I daresay she's the most experienced of us all."

If glares could smite, Ravenwood would no longer have had a wife to worry about.

As it happened, Simmons was so flustered by his master's arrival that he trod upon his mistress's toe, thus distracting the both of them from noticing whether or not Ravenwood's stony visage remotely indicated a desire to waltz in a sitting room at half ten in the morning.

Very well.

With an exaggerated sigh that went completely unnoticed, he strode forward and led Mrs. Havens into a waltz.

Despite the lack of orchestra or bared floorboards, she surprised him by matching him with perfect fluidity and grace.

At his raised eyebrow, she let out a cackle. "Just because I married a parson doesn't mean he didn't know how to…dance."

Ravenwood tried his best to maintain a blank expression.

"It's true," Katherine called out gaily. "Great-Uncle Havens was my very first dance instructor. I credit him fully with the success of my season."

Success? By what standard?

"You failed to bring a single suitor up to scratch," he pointed out dryly.

"That's what made it a success," she said with a grin. "I was not in the market for fools. I managed to avoid leg-shackling myself to one. Thus, a resounding success."

Ravenwood considered her words. His wife had avoided marrying a fool, which meant she did not consider him to be one.

He, on the other hand, felt every bit the fool. Dancing in the parlor without music or good sense. His ears heated and he gritted his teeth. It wasn't quite as dreadful as making a public spectacle of himself, but it was uncomfortable enough for him to ease the elderly Mrs. Havens from his arms and put a stop to this madness. He was a duke, and ought to act like one.

"Simmons," he said in a voice that brooked no argument.

His butler flushed scarlet and released Katherine from their waltz with almost comical haste. "Your grace."

Ravenwood inclined his head. "You may resume your post."

Simmons all but fled out the door.

Ravenwood had half a mind to do the same. Waltzing in

the parlor in the middle of the morning? Katherine had him at sixes and sevens. He *abhorred* being at sixes and sevens.

His mind ached. What he needed was a visit to his garden to collect himself. A retreat into peaceful solitude never failed to restore his equilibrium.

Then again... He slanted a sidelong look at his wife.

Sunlight streamed through the windows, bathing her in warm morning light. Her color was still high from the excitement of the moment, giving her cheeks a rosy flush. The earlier carefree smile was no longer upon her lips, but her clear blue eyes watched him with open interest, rather than petulance for having ruined her fun.

That was her nature, he realized. Open to anything. Happy with everything. Passionate. Always ready for life's next adventure.

That was not at all who Ravenwood was. Yet he could not help but admire her spirit. Solitude might be his preferred escape, but it was likely to bring Katherine more pain than peace. He could not have that.

"It is a beautiful day," he said gruffly. "Care to take a turn about the grounds with me?"

Her eyes shone, and a smile blossomed on her face once more. "I would love to."

He turned to Mrs. Havens. "Madam—"

She shook her head. "My old legs are too tired for more exercise. You two enjoy yourselves. I have plenty of needlework to entertain me."

"As you wish." He offered his arm to Katherine. "Shall we?"

She looped her fingers about the crook of his elbow. "Absolutely."

After sending a servant to fetch a bonnet and pelisse for Katherine, Ravenwood returned her hand to his arm and led her down one of the many walking paths.

The trimmed hedges and squared corners lacked the wild beauty of his secret garden, but their artificial perfection made Ravenwood House famous for being one of the loveliest walking estates in London. The grounds were frequently visited by spectators seeking to stroll the famed paths firsthand.

He chided himself. He shouldn't have allowed his natural reticence to prevent him from enjoying Katherine's company out-of-doors.

Come to think of it, he was surprised she wasn't out here every day herself, entertaining her friends. Perhaps she did not realize she was free to do so.

"Do you like the walking paths?" he asked.

"Very much," she replied, sending him a smile that warmed him as much as the sun. "Everything I see is magnificent."

His neck heated in pleasure. She was not looking at the garden, but at him.

He had to fight a powerful desire to pull her into his arms and kiss her. The paths were far too public for such a spectacle.

"I cannot help but notice you have not yet had any visitors," he said instead. "Please know that you are welcome to invite whomever you wish at any time."

Surprise flitted across her eyes. "I would have expected you to prohibit such a thing. Or did you forget my friends are as likely to be actors and violinists as they are to be barons and countesses? I'm sure you've read the papers."

"This is your home," he said simply. "You will forgive me if I choose not to entertain even the Regent himself, but you are every bit as free to fill your schedule with as many guests as you like."

She was silent for a long moment, then shook her head. "I believe my theatre acquaintances are as unlikely to drop by for tea as Lady Jersey would be. Everyone is more comfortable in their own environment. I like mad crushes of people. I cannot recall the last time I went for a stroll with a single person. Except for you and Aunt Havens, of course."

She lifted a shoulder. "I may know half of London, but I would consider none a bosom friend."

His eyes widened. Although he himself could count his friends on one hand, they were as dear to him as siblings, and had known him for almost as long as his own sister.

That an introverted gentleman should often find himself lonely, he accepted as fact. That Katherine should feel alone despite thousands of acquaintances stunned him. He slanted her a closer look.

Perhaps when she'd said that everyone felt most comfortable in their own environment, she was not speaking of barons and actresses, but herself.

She had not visited her museum since becoming his wife. He had taken her away from her townhouse. Upbraided her for daring to claim a single room as her own. This was *not* her home, as he so frequently claimed. This was *his* home. His environment.

It was up to him to let her in.

"You may have the east wing," he said suddenly. This *was* her environment now. He would make it so.

"What?" She blinked up at him in confusion. "I don't understand."

"You deserve not a single room, but rather half of all that is mine. With the exception of the family parlor, you may do with the east wing as you please."

She stared at him. "Even if I were to fill every inch with mummies and scarabs?"

"Ravenwood House is ours to share. If you wish your half to be a showcase for antiquities, that is your prerogative."

"My half," she repeated, her voice faraway. "All right."

His brow furrowed. He had meant the gesture to be inclusive, expansive. To make her feel at home. To show he cared. But by splitting the estate into wholly separate halves, had he only succeeded in dividing them further?

His temples pounded in frustration. He was not *good* at

knowing what to say. Especially not whilst in the moment.

With his journal open and an entire afternoon before him, he could craft poetry that expressed his innermost thoughts with every syllable. But with the sun at his back and his wife on his arm, the best he could do to welcome her to her new home was to blurt nonsense about delineating the divide between them even further.

No. It was not the best he could do. There was one place that was so private, so sacred, so *his*, that he did not even allow his servants within its walls. It was his paradise. His heart. His secret.

It was time to invite Katherine into his private garden.

Chapter Thirteen

Ravenwood forced his shoulders to relax so as not to betray how deeply he feared the risk he was about to take.

His garden was more than a secret. It was the one place he could truly be himself. A place that belonged only to him. Inside its walls, both he and nature were free from society's stringent rules and disapproving gaze.

There were no neatly trimmed hedges, no manicured corners, no painted walking paths.

The great stone wall surrounding the garden was as tall and imposing as Ravenwood House itself, but inside was a wonderland of delicate scents and untamed beauty.

The trees grew as tall as they wished, in any direction they pleased. The flowers were not segregated in this section or that, but rather allowed to grow wild, flourishing in an ocean of riotous color rather than each species confined to small, defined squares.

This was where Ravenwood felt most alive. Where he was most vulnerable.

The one place he was truly himself.

He kept his eyes on the pebbled path before them. "I…have a garden."

She nodded. "In the rear of the property."

Surprise drew him up short. "You knew?"

But of course she did. He had personally instructed his staff to deny her nothing. He was the only one who hadn't followed his own directive.

He rubbed the back of his neck. "If you have no pressing engagements, perhaps you would like to visit it now?"

Her face lit with surprise and pleasure. "I would love to."

His mouth dried. "Then it would be my great pleasure to take you there."

That, of course, was a blatant falsehood. He didn't want to take anyone there.

Yet Katherine, of all people, was the most likely to understand why he found it beautiful and peaceful.

If for some reason she did not, if she found it silly and gauche, her derision would haunt the walls. Every time he thought of his secret garden, his sacred place, he would remember her rejection and no longer be able to find peace within.

Even if she liked the garden, she might not understand it. Might not understand *him*. And his tongue would be too tied to convey how he felt.

He searched for something, anything, to erase his growing nervousness as they neared his private garden.

"I notice you have not visited your museum of late."

She bit her lip. "You're correct. I've relinquished all daily duties to a competent overseer whilst I focus on my next project."

"Introducing artists to patrons?"

"It's more than that." A bounce of excitement crept into her step. "Yes, patronage is important, but so is developing an environment where one needn't hide their artistic inclinations. Scholars of both genders have the Bluestocking Society. Why shouldn't there also be a Performing and Creative Arts Society, open to everyone?"

"You're not planning an event," he said with sudden clarity. "You're hoping to start a movement. Create a community."

She touched her fingers to her chest. "My dream is not only to spread awareness and interest in the arts, but to foster them. Improve them. Strengthen them. Anyone can sponsor anyone else. A place where poets can chat with earls and marchionesses can talk to actresses without their economic backgrounds preventing a connection—*that* is a community."

"Poets?" he echoed, as casually as he could.

Until this moment, he hadn't believed she would hold such a solitary endeavor in as high esteem as she held acting and music.

She waved a hand. "I just said that as an example. Every third dandy believes himself the next Lord Byron." She rolled her eyes with a laugh. "None of them would know good poetry if it bit them in the nose."

His chest tightened. He was careful to betray nothing.

"In order to make the inaugural event the greatest success possible, what I really need are stunning entertainers. Actors, acrobats, jugglers, musicians, dancers. Astonishing, visceral performances that cannot help but open hearts or purses."

He could not deny that such an event could easily have London abuzz. "It seems you've thought of everything."

"I've tried to." She smiled up at him.

He was dubious a single gala would snowball into a serious community, but had no doubt the opening event itself would be just as astonishing as Katherine hoped. Everything she planned turned out better than expected.

He had a longstanding distrust of change, because every time his life forked into a new direction, new troubles came with it. Inheriting a title meant the loss of his parents. Gaining a guardian meant the destruction of his home. Staying home from war to manage his dukedom meant watching his best friends return broken and bitter men.

Time had also brought them better fortune, in the end.

His friends had suffered great losses, but they'd ultimately gained love and peace.

He hoped the same would eventually happen for him. That was why he was leading Katherine off the carefully cultivated public paths and along the dirt trail leading to his private garden.

She stared up in obvious awe at the great stone wall protecting his private refuge. "Is this a garden or a castle?"

"Both," he answered simply. The moat was the dukedom surrounding the walls. The inner sanctum was where nature reigned, and he was its humble servant.

Heretical thoughts. He paused with his key in the lock. His palms were sweating. This was a terrible idea. He was giving up his privacy. His solitude. His sanctuary.

Katherine's fingers tightened about his arm and she leaned closer in anticipation.

He twisted the key in the lock and pushed open the heavy iron door.

Happiness filled him at the familiar sight of his private garden. Enormous trees with wide, leafy branches provided plenty of shade from the morning sun. A profusion of varying flowers rippled in the breeze like colorful fish in a sea of green.

So much ivy covered the interior side of the stone walls that the garden appeared not closed off, but rather endless, as if they were surrounded only by untamed hills of grass and flowers.

Katherine's mouth fell open in wonder. She clutched her hands to her chest and spun in a slow circle, her wide blue eyes drinking in every wild, unclipped section. The grass tugged at the lace hem of her day dress, but she seemed too entranced by the view to even notice.

She turned bright eyes toward him, her mouth parting as if he were just coming into focus. "Did *you* do this?"

"I did nothing," he said. "Like many things, nature is at its most beautiful when we don't try to control it."

She stared at him for a heartbeat and then threw her arms about his neck and rose up on her toes. "What an incredibly poetic thing to say."

He couldn't help it. He kissed her.

This time was different. He wasn't kissing her because she was his bride and therefore he was obligated to. Nor was he kissing her for base, lusty reasons—although it was true that he had never stopped wanting her.

This kiss was because she was Katherine. Because here, he was not a duke, but Lawrence Pembroke, the man. The poet. The seeker of beauty.

And he had found it.

This kiss was because Katherine loved his lawless garden that by polite standards was not a garden at all. It was a wild thing. Lush and savage. Blossoms and thorns.

This kiss was because she saw *him.* Saw him in the peonies and the cherry trees, in the ivy and the twisting branches.

He kissed her because he wanted to. Needed to. Yearned for her. This garden wasn't a mere hideaway—it was an extension of himself. He was every bird, every leaf. By letting her within its walls, he had let her into his heart.

Katherine was perhaps the one person who *wouldn't* find his unconventional side a detriment. She didn't care what society thought. If life wasn't how she wished, she simply made it so. She was free. As wild as the sea of flowers around them. And as impossible to ever truly tame.

Gasping, he pulled away before he fell so far into their kiss that he would never find his way back home.

She slid an arm about him and leaned her head against his chest. The pounding of his heart had to be deafening. He wrapped an arm about her waist and nestled his cheek against the top of her head.

"You are like a dahlia," he said softly.

She tilted her head up slightly. "Which one is that?"

He pointed with his free hand. "The gold ones are

here... The pink ones there... The orange ones over there. Dahlias are more than pretty. They're strong and resilient. And new to my garden this year."

"They're beautiful," she breathed. "And they're all so different."

"Just like you." He plucked a small golden dahlia from its stem and tucked it behind her ear. She looked like a wood nymph, capable of seducing the coldest heart and then disappearing into the mist.

"Thank you." She snuggled close. "I love your garden."

He nodded, pleased.

She made him happy and gave him hope.

Chapter Fourteen

Kate swept into her great-aunt's sitting room on a cloud of giddy romance.

Aunt Havens clucked her tongue at the sight of the dahlia at Kate's ear and the grass stains upon her hem. "Never say you left him behind to run off amongst the flowers."

Grinning, Kate shook her head and swirled about the room. "The opposite, Aunt. He whisked *me* off the walking path and into his hidden paradise."

Aunt Havens raised her brows in surprise. "That *is* unexpected."

Kate clasped her hands together. Ravenwood was much more than she had dreamed.

The moment she'd realized how deeply his garden mattered to him—that he'd fully expected its unconventional wildness to fall short in her eyes, yet he'd bared it to her anyway—she had irrevocably fallen for him.

What was not to love? His private garden was both his secret and his heart, and he literally opened it up to let her inside.

He had the soul of a poet. *She* was the one who had been blind to his beauty.

Guilt assailed her as she recalled how carelessly she had

dismissed him, before they had even met. She had developed a casual contempt toward him based on nothing more than his title and impeccable reputation.

She had assumed there was nothing more to him than what he presented to society, and judged him without a second thought. She had been wrong.

He lived in the same world she did. He simply confronted it a different way. Outwardly, he became the most proper duke to grace England's soil.

Behind closed walls, he was drawn in a different direction. He did not allow society to dictate how he spent his private moments. When the world got too frustrating, he escaped into a secret jungle in his own backyard.

And he'd invited her in.

She pulled the dahlia from her ear and pressed it to her chest. "I could love him someday, Aunt."

"Could you?" Aunt Havens' smile brightened.

Kate gazed down at the dahlia and thought about her future.

Ravenwood was wonderful. He was smart. Romantic. She didn't know how he felt, what he might think or say. He didn't give his approbation lightly, which increased its value all the more.

She cared about his opinion. Everyone else liked her, but she wasn't certain they necessarily *respected* her—or her ideas. His respect would mean more than anyone else's. His love would mean the world.

"He gave me this dahlia." She held it out for her aunt to see. "He says it reminds him of me."

"Because you're beautiful," Aunt Havens guessed.

"Because I'm different." Kate gazed at the exotic flower as she remembered the warmth in his eyes.

Debutantes were expected to adhere to the same rules, to follow the same fashions, to mimic each other in comportment and desires.

She had been complimented on her French dresses and

perfect ringlets her entire life, but no one had ever told her what they most appreciated about her was that she was *different* from the others. Until today.

If she'd had any skill at all with watercolor, she would paint this beautiful flower to remember the moment forever.

The day she'd discovered herself falling wholly and irreversibly in love.

She might be like a dahlia, but he was like his secret garden. Tall and imposing, with great stone walls and a locked iron gate to keep others out. Wild, untamed beauty within.

A smile that felt like sunshine upon her soul.

They could *not* get an annulment. She would stay married to him no matter what it took. Even if that meant someday having his child. Or trying to.

She brought the dahlia to her chest and closed her eyes. Terror gripped her.

Ravenwood was not an unreasonable man. He'd invited her into his garden. Surely he would understand her need to be intimate with him for the first few times without the specter of childbirth casting its shadow over the marriage bed.

He was a duke. He had resources beyond her imagination. He would not let anything happen to her—or their baby. She opened her eyes and nodded firmly.

Next year would be soon enough to think about children.

She crossed the room to the bell pull in order to ring for a vase. Her mind was already planning where to place the dahlia so that she would see it every morning when she woke and every night before falling asleep.

Even when Ravenwood was too busy to spend time with her, she would be able to look at the dahlia and remember how it had felt to kiss him in his garden.

When she turned back around, Aunt Havens was on her knees, peering beneath the chairs and side tables.

Kate strode forward, frowning. "Did you lose something, Aunt?"

"I'm afraid so." Aunt Havens let out a deep sigh of frustration. "I can't find that dog anywhere!"

Kate's smile wobbled. The blasted dog again. This was the second time in as many weeks.

There had to be something Kate could do. Playing along wasn't working. Nor did explaining the dog had long since died. What Aunt Havens might need was a new dog. A real one.

And perhaps what Kate needed…was Ravenwood.

Chapter Fifteen

After spending a delightful afternoon with Katherine in the garden, the last thing Ravenwood wanted to do was set off for Parliament and spend the next eight hours shuttered inside the Palace of Westminster with the House of Lords.

But he was a duke who knew his duty, so as much as he might have preferred to stay home and see what the evening might bring, his country needed him. The ridiculous Coinage Committee needed him.

As much as he hated being cooped up with so many people, so many voices, he often feared the whole system would fall apart if he were not present to herd the lordlings back into line every time they strayed off course and out of hand.

Tonight, however, instead of suffering through the usual anxiety of what to say and how to say it, his mind kept slipping back to his garden. The fear of rejection, the relief of acceptance, the joy that had filled them both so vividly that she'd thrown herself into his arms and—

"Wouldn't you say, Ravenwood?"

"Er…" Ravenwood blinked at dozens of curious faces. Heat climbed up his neck at the unexpected attention. "I would need to…consult some figures."

"You and your figures, Ravenwood!"

The men turned from him to begin arguing amongst themselves again.

He rubbed his face and forced himself to pay attention. Just a little while longer. These meetings rarely went later than one or two in the morning. Katherine was infamous for going out every evening. She would still be awake when he got home.

Except she wasn't.

No light shone beneath the crack of their adjoining door. She was in bed, asleep.

Come to think of it, she hadn't gone out a single time since becoming his wife. No theatres, no dinner parties, not even a stroll in St. James Square. He frowned.

Was she unhappy? Was it his fault?

Pensive, he maintained his habitual silence as his valet removed his boots and dress clothes and prepared his bed.

Until that afternoon, he had never explicitly given Katherine permission to do as she pleased, in or out of Ravenwood House. In all honesty, it had never occurred to him that explicit permission would be necessary. She was his duchess. A duchess could do as she liked.

More to the point: she was *Katherine*. Katherine always did as she pleased.

Or did she?

He sat on the edge of his bed and cast a long, speculative gaze at the closed door standing between them.

This union had not been in either of their plans. However, in Ravenwood's case, he had always *wanted* to get married. To have a wife, children, a family. To find love.

On their wedding night, Katherine had made it perfectly clear that she did not share those sentiments. She had not longed for a husband, least of all Ravenwood. And she certainly wasn't delighted to bear his children. She wasn't willing to entertain the idea at all.

Which left them with what? He leaned back onto his bed and stared up at the tester.

The one thing *he* wasn't willing to risk was a chance at love. Their wedding night had proven that she felt physical desire for him. This afternoon in the garden had proven that they could connect at a deeper level.

She might not have chosen him at first—but if he gave her time and space, there was still a chance that she might.

He didn't want her to simply accept his presence in her bedchamber. He wanted her to *want* him. All of him. His mind, his body, his heart. He wanted her to want to create a family together just as badly as he did. He wanted them to *be* a family. Partners in life and love.

He also wasn't a saint...or a fool. It was possible that their marriage might become the sort of union he'd always yearned for—and it was just as possible that it would not.

He rolled on his side to face away from the adjoining door.

For the next several weeks, he would be too busy with the House of Lords to do much courting, even in his own home. He could afford to give Katherine a month to adjust to her new role, but he would not pine for his wife from no more than a few feet away. The dukedom required an heir.

If she was not ready to come to him by the time the Season ended, he would go to her.

They would either become a family...or end their marriage for good.

Chapter Sixteen

Kate awoke exhausted, due to a fitful night.

Her pillows were the most comfortable she'd ever experienced, her mattress and blankets luxurious, but all she could think about was Ravenwood. Once again, he hadn't come to her bedchamber.

He was either too busy with the House of Lords...or too uninterested. She tried not to think about that possibility. Until Parliament adjourned, the best thing she could do to stay sane was to keep herself occupied.

She had the Society of Creative and Performing Arts to plan. An aunt to look after.

A husband to yearn for.

She refreshed the water for the vase on her windowsill and bent her head to the dahlia. It smelled like sunshine and secret gardens. Its golden petals made her long to relive every one of his kisses.

To bolster her spirits, she forced her mind away from her absent husband and onto planning her final event of the Season. She was excited to pick a date and a venue and work on creating an opening night grander than any other theatre had ever managed. Ravenwood had promised to attend. It had to be perfect.

She hurried with her morning ablution, intending to

pause for nothing more than a quick bite of toasted bread before being on her way. If she dallied any longer, Aunt Havens might decide to accompany her.

While Kate loved her great-aunt more dearly than anyone else in the world, Aunt Havens was more of a distraction than help. Kate needed to use every ounce of charisma she possessed to convince the caliber of perform-ers she had in mind to put on a free show...and then to convince the *ton* to respond the way she had in mind.

Debutantes could sing in musicales, but not in operas—and why not? At least they should be able to *speak* to one another. A lady was expected to be competent in watercolor and embroidery, but to leave set painting and costume design to the vulgar masses. Nonsense! Singers were singers and artists were artists.

The Society for Creative and Performing Arts was a wonderful opportunity for the *beau monde* to explore their interests and passions with the people who had the most experience with them.

And then they could open their pocketbooks to enable emerging artists to live their dreams.

Kate dashed into the breakfast room and drew up short when she realized the table was currently occupied.

Not by Aunt Havens.

Ravenwood.

Just the sight of him brought back the scent of flowers and fresh grass, the sun on her face, the feel of his arm nestled about her to hold her close.

And their kiss.

"Good morning." He rose to his feet and bowed.

She curtsied and slid into the chair opposite him, her earlier haste forgotten.

"You're up early." His words were casual, but his green eyes drank her in as if he'd been prepared to wait for her all morning.

Her stomach flipped. She hadn't stopped thinking of

him for a single moment. "I'm to make progress on my project today. Or at least, I had been. If you're home today, we could..."

He was already shaking his head. "I've meetings all day, I'm afraid. Go ahead and do as you please. I won't have much free time until Parliament ends."

Until Parliament ends. She nodded dully. That was weeks away.

"Tell me about your project," he said. "It sounds...fun. How will you begin?"

Her mouth quirked as she realized that no part of planning, executing, or attending an intricate, crowded event would sound like fun to Ravenwood.

She was lucky he would be present at all. He would no doubt have preferred to spend the entirety of the night locked in his garden, had she not begged him to lend his support by being the first to offer patronage. She smiled at him.

"I plan to start with the performers," she explained as a footman served her breakfast.

No, not "a" footman, she reminded herself. This one was John. He could not eat cheese without becoming ill. He had worked here for seven and a half years.

She knew because his details were written on page one hundred and thirty of the fifth "lower servants" journal the previous mistress of Ravenwood House had kept.

Lady Amelia had been kind enough to send over her own notes, which turned out to be an incredibly daunting quantity of meticulously indexed and cross-referenced journals, compiled over the years in Lady Amelia's own small, precise hand.

Kate had read every single page and made her own list of what she felt were the most important elements, as well as notations on where in Lady Amelia's journals more information could be found.

It would take a lifetime to become half as fluent in the

daily inner workings as Lady Amelia had been, but Kate no longer felt lost—or incompetent. Between her notes and Lady Amelia's, Kate was slowly gaining her confidence.

Things might take a little more time as she got used to how everything worked, but someday, running Ravenwood House would be as easy as opening a museum or starting an arts society.

She hoped.

In her scant free time, she would do her best to move forward with the Society for Creative and Performing Arts.

"Today I will begin spreading the word to actors, acrobats, opera singers, and the like. They are by far the most important element, so they have to come first."

"Aren't the donors you're hoping to attract also a key component?" He raised his brows.

She waved a hand. "Money is easy. Art is hard. The easiest way to get the *ton* involved is simply to tell them everyone else already is. They are sheep. They'll follow."

Ravenwood choked politely behind his cup of tea. "I hope your attempts at persuasion are a little more delicate when you speak to your 'sheep' in person."

Her cheeks flushed. He was right. She had spoken thoughtlessly. A trait she was trying to correct.

"It's a Society of the Creative and Performing Arts," she tried to explain. "It can't be a Society of the Creative and Performing Arts without creative and performing artists."

"It also can't function without funding," he pointed out. "I could offer a Ravenwood Grant tomorrow. A hundred pounds each to the first ten sopranos who walk in the door. How many do you think would show up on the front lawn?"

"If all I wanted was to rain money at random individuals," she said in frustration, "I would take your thousand pounds and toss it from the balcony at the nearest orchestra. That is *not* a society, and not at all what I'm trying to build."

"I know. That's what I'm trying to show *you*." He put

down his tea. "If you want the *ton* to feel like they're part of something new, something valuable, then you must treat them that way, too. If you want to do the impossible and have jugglers rub elbows with earls, all parts of the whole are equally important." He paused. "Except you, of course."

Her mouth fell open. "Not me?"

"You're the most important of all. You're not just the brain behind the organization, you're its face, its heart, and its soul." His eyes were filled with pride. "You're also the one person I truly believe not only *could* make something like this happen…but undoubtedly will."

Her belly fluttered. He wasn't belittling her project. He wanted her to succeed as much as she did. Took for granted that it would be a triumphant victory.

She reconsidered his recommendation on how to view the patrons.

Her arms tucked about her waist. He was right. Moving within society's rules did not mean giving up her goals. It meant achieving them a different way. Possibly even a better way.

"Thank you," she said as she rose to her feet. He had given her the right attitude with which to face her day. "If you like, I will keep you apprised of my progress."

He rose to his feet as well. "I would like that very much."

She curtsied and hurried out of the room to fetch her pelisse. She was still thinking about him when the coach pulled up at the theatre. Ravenwood had surprised her yet again. His support of her ideas, his willingness to help… He was a wonderful husband. No wonder she could never get him out of her mind.

"Lady K!" crowed a dozen voices as she stepped behind the stage curtain. "*Your grace*, that is. Hard to believe you're a duchess now!"

She grinned at her friends. It had been too long since last she'd seen them.

"Tell us," Miss Nottingworth said with a wiggle of her eyebrows. "Was that stolen kiss worth it?"

"How could it be?" Mr. Devonshire laughed, as he slapped an arm about Kate's shoulders. "Like the lady always says, the Frost Fair is never over when you're anywhere near Ravenwood!"

Bile churned in Kate's stomach at the sound of her own careless words thrown back to her.

The cruel things she had said when she hadn't even taken the time to get to know him now haunted her. Her unfounded prejudice against him was unforgivable.

"He's nothing like that," she said urgently. "He's kind and caring and thoughtful—"

"He's a stick-in-the-mud. You said so yourself." Mr. Devonshire shook his head. "How could someone like you possibly be happy with someone like that?"

"It's impossible." Miss Nottingworth crossed her arms. "He doesn't know you. He couldn't."

"He does," Kate insisted. It was true. His support had proved it.

Miss Nottingworth raised a skeptical brow. "What was his wedding gift?"

The east wing, Kate started to say, then changed her mind. He'd given her something even better.

"A beautiful garden," she answered with pride. Happiness radiated through her chest. Those few moments had meant everything.

"Not bad," Miss Nottingworth admitted grudgingly.

Mr. Devonshire raised his brows. "And what did you give him in return?"

Kate stared back at the set designer in dawning horror. Her stomach bottomed. *Nothing*. Not even a wedding night.

"I…" She floundered for a response.

Mr. Devonshire laughed and shook his head. "Just quizzing you. What could anyone give a duke who has everything?"

What indeed. Her belly fluttered. There were a few things Ravenwood didn't have and desperately wanted. One might make the perfect wedding gift.

Kate had ruined things once when she'd filled his parents' empty parlor with her Egyptian artifacts. Not this time. She was in the unique position of having the precise connections to turn a faded memory back into reality.

Mr. Devonshire had been the most sought-after woodworker in all of London. She had no doubt he could recreate every stick of custom carved furniture in that painting so precisely that even Ravenwood wouldn't be able to tell the difference.

Miss Nottingworth was the most talented costume designer in England. She would be able to replicate every fabric, every design, right down to the thread.

Her mad idea wasn't a dream—it was something she could turn into reality!

If Kate managed such a feat, perhaps Ravenwood would realize how much she wanted their marriage to succeed. That it *must* succeed. Her heart was already his.

She wished she had a secret garden of her own, just so she could invite him to share it with her. He might think of her as a dahlia, but he was the one with hidden beauty. She longed to be able to ease some of the hurt from his past. To show him she was on his side. That they *did* have a future together.

Kate's tight shoulders loosened. Soon he would see how deeply she cared. If all of her contacts worked together, they could bring the parlor back to life in a matter of weeks.

But to do so... She swallowed.

First, they would need the painting.

Chapter Seventeen

Kate paced the halls of Ravenwood House in a cold sweat.

She desperately wanted to surprise her husband with a complete recreation of his childhood parlor, but to do so, she could neither allow woodworkers and designers and seamstresses to use the parlor as their workshop, nor could she allow them to keep the cherished portrait in their own workshop for weeks on end.

Even if the gift were not a surprise, Ravenwood would never allow the parlor to be invaded in such a way—or to allow the painting out of his possession for even a moment.

So she'd made a compromise. A risky one. She'd snuck the family portrait to her friends whilst Ravenwood was at Parliament and instructed them to return it the following night when he was away again.

Twenty-four hours for the best painter of their acquaintance to forge a copy of the canvas with perfect exactitude.

Twenty-four hours in which Ravenwood might decide at any moment to revisit his old memories…and discover them missing.

Three hours remained. Ravenwood was still at home. The portrait was not.

Kate's fingernails were bitten to nubs.

She hadn't stepped outside of the house since the painting had left the manor. She had to be on hand to intercept it the moment it returned. She also had to be on hand to intercept Ravenwood, should he venture anywhere near the parlor.

Distract him with what? She wasn't certain. Something. Anything. It didn't matter. Soon, the painting would be back in its proper place and she could breathe again. Soon after, once the parlor had been brought back to life, her husband would see how much she cared.

Their marriage might have been an accident, but it wasn't a mistake. Not if they worked at it. Ravenwood eschewed artsy nonsense whereas she adored it, but that did not mean they couldn't come to love each other. For them to live *together*, instead as two solitary souls haunting separate halves of a sprawling, lifeless manor.

Where *was* her husband, anyway?

She strolled by his bedchamber as casually as possible. The valet was alone. Ravenwood had not yet arrived to dress for the parliamentary meeting. Nor was he in the dining area.

His office, then. The only other room he ever visited.

Kate shook her head. She could not imagine how boring life would be if it were filled with nothing but work and duty. She knew from her cousin's example that the other peers of the realm did not leave one eight-hour parliamentary session only to spend another eight going over the same material alone.

How Ravenwood could endure spending so much time at his desk was beyond her.

She wrapped her arms about her chest. Light spilled from the open doorway to his office.

He was seated at his desk, his head bent over one of his many ledgers, a pen poised over one of the blank pages. His chestnut curls spilled over his forehead. Concentration lined his handsome face. Her heart thumped at the sight.

She paused in the corridor to watch.

He didn't move.

Seconds turned into minutes. If it weren't for the occasional blink of his eyes, a casual observer might have believed him a statue carved of wax. She couldn't even distinguish his breathing.

Suddenly, he jerked the pen away from the blank page and stabbed it viciously into a pot of ink.

For several long moments, he tapped the nub against the inkwell to remove excess ink, dipped the tip into the ink again as if too much had slid away, then started the process of tapping and dunking all over again.

At last, he returned to his original position, with his pen once again hovering over a blank page.

He didn't move.

Neither did she.

After a long moment, something changed. His eyes softened. The corners of his lips quirked into a wistful smile. And his pen flew across the page so rapidly that he barely took time to do more than dash the tip into the ink before letting it sail across the page again and again as if he were a man possessed.

Mystified, she stepped forward. "What are you writing?"

"Poetry." He slammed the journal closed without allowing the ink to dry. His tone was flat. His face, expressionless.

Her mouth fell open in surprise. Poetry? *Him?* "May I—"

"No." He threw the thick blue volume into a drawer and turned a key in the lock. "It is private. As is this office."

Her face flamed with heat. Not because he had chastised her for spying on his private space. But because she had judged him incapable of such an interest.

Once again, she had been wrong.

His poetry might be wonderful or terrible or anything in between, but it was sincere and it was *his*.

"Pray continue," she stammered, backing into the hall. "As you may recall, I've the Grenville soirée tonight and ought to select my gown."

Before he could stop her—not that he showed any sign of wishing to do so—she flung herself out of sight and pressed her back into the corridor wall. Her heart refused to slow.

Her husband was a poet.

The Duke of Ravenwood was a *poet*.

She squeezed her eyes shut. All this time he'd let her blather on about her creative friends, and he *was* one.

He wasn't just romantic when inside the walls of his secret garden—he was expressive and imaginative in the privacy of his mind.

And he had gazed at her in his typical stoic silence when she'd casually dismissed poetry as featherbrained fops playacting at being Byron.

In horror, she clapped her hands over her mouth to bite back a hysterical laugh.

When was the last time *she'd* written a poem or danced a ballet or sang an operetta? Never. The last time was never. Her chest tightened.

He'd had every opportunity to throw her closemindedness in her face. Yet he'd chosen not to do so. He was too admirable for that.

If he wanted privacy to exercise his creativity, she would do everything in her power to give him as much freedom as he required.

Heart thudding, she pushed away from the wainscoting and made her way back toward her half of the manor. Toward the empty parlor, where she would await the painting.

From now on, she would keep to the east wing unless explicitly invited to join him elsewhere. His office was his. The west wing was his. The garden was his. From now on, she would make it her duty to ensure he was never interrupted when he was in any of those places.

She had asked him to sponsor an artist at her inaugural event. Well, she would sponsor *him*.

He didn't lack for money, or materials, or a workspace. What the overworked, under-appreciated Duke of Ravenwood most needed was time to himself. Time to *be* himself. The luxury of a few hours here and there where his presence or signature or advice or leadership was not required by someone else.

A chance to be a poet. To enjoy his garden. To experience a moment of freedom. To just…be.

"Your grace? A package has arrived for you."

Her pulse skipped. She whirled around to see a footman bearing a large, flat crate. Thank heavens!

"Please place it outside my aunt's bedchamber." That sounded innocuous enough. A heavy sigh of relief escaped her lungs.

Now the only trick would be smuggling the portrait out of the crate and back onto the wall.

She had asked the maids who cleaned that corridor not to enter the parlor for a few days, just in case the painting hadn't returned in time, but that was no guarantee that curiosity at the strange request wouldn't propel one of them to peek around the corner.

She hung back just long enough to give the footman time to drop off the crate and walk away before rushing to Aunt Havens' guest quarters to retrieve the package.

With the aid of a small knife she'd sequestered just for this purpose, she was able to pry off the lid and slide out the linen-wrapped frame.

Her nerves jumped. Before anyone else could chance upon her, she hurried straight to the back parlor. She didn't unwrap the frame until she was standing directly in front of the empty nails where the portrait had once hung.

Carefully, she placed it back on the wall then stood back to rake it over with a critical eye.

It *looked* the same. No visible nicks in the gilded frame, no dirt or stains upon the cracked canvas.

She narrowed her eyes as an insidious thought occurred to her. This had better be the original portrait and not the forged copy. A painter like her friend would be talented enough to duplicate every brushstroke, cracks and all.

No. She shook her head. Her friends would not have done that. Their artistic fingers might be capable of such deception, but their kind hearts were not. They wanted Kate's gift to succeed as much as she did.

She folded up the empty linen as if it were no more than a bit of mending and slipped back through the corridors to her aunt's bedchamber.

The empty crate had been removed from the hallway. In its place stood an extravagantly coiffed Aunt Havens, outfitted in canary yellow silk from neck to toe.

"What time are we leaving?" she asked. "Aren't you going to put on a proper gown?"

Kate blinked. The Grenville soirée. She'd nearly forgot.

Aunt Havens had not, of course. She loved parties as much as Kate did, and had attended them all as her chaperone since the moment of her come-out.

Kate grinned back at her aunt.

Now that she was married and no longer required chaperonage, she still couldn't imagine going anywhere without Aunt Havens.

Her aunt had never been a simple duenna, but rather Kate's favorite person and closest friend. The most amusing rout was made even more fun by having Aunt Havens at her side to make jests to and confide secrets.

"Of course I'll wear a proper gown," she said gaily, looping her arm through her aunt's. "Come help me choose one that won't clash with yours. I had thought cobalt at first, but now I'm starting to think, why not a mint green?"

Now that the portrait was back and she and Aunt Havens had diverting plans, Kate's spirits lightened considerably.

No more risks. No more prejudice. A heightened sense of responsibility. She was New Kate. Duchess of Ravenwood, in fact. From now on, she would act like it.

The moment she was bathed and dressed, she and Aunt Havens set off for the Grenville soiree.

Kate had intended to take her husband's practical advice to heart, and started to woo potential patrons to her opening gala with the same enthusiasm and respect she'd given to the performers and artists.

"Miss Grenville," she said when she caught up with the eldest Grenville sibling. "I quite enjoyed your family musicale a few months back."

"That's fortunate," Miss Grenville said with a wry smile. "I am pleased to inform you that it was our last."

"Pleased?" Kate stared at her, disappointment curving her shoulders. "I thought you loved music."

"I adore hearing it far more than performing it," Miss Grenville confessed. "Now that I am of age, I shall spend as much of my time as possible watching the stage, rather than standing on it."

Kate's spine straightened. "If that is the case, you and your family may be interested to take part in the upcoming Society for the Creative and Performing Arts."

Miss Grenville shook her head. "I meant what I said about no longer singing for a crowd."

"Nor would you have to. This society will bring together art enthusiasts with practitioners. You would be able to sponsor the singer or singers of your choice, and become a *patron* of the arts, rather than a performer."

Miss Grenville frowned. "Do you mean...sponsor an opera singer like Angelica Catalini?"

"Not a famous one," Kate corrected. "A *soon*-to-be famous one. Someone extremely talented who, without your help and patronage, would never be destined for greatness. Years from now, when audiences are clamoring for tickets to hear the greatest soprano in London, it could be because *you* discovered her at the Society for Creative and Performing Arts and paved her way to fame."

"Me, a patron of the arts?" Miss Grenville's eyes shone. "What a lovely idea! I cannot wait to tell Mother. I am certain every member of our family will wish to sponsor an artist. Is there any limit?"

"No limit at all. Please spread the word to anyone you think might be interested." Happiness soared through Kate's veins. "With everyone's help, London's arts and theatre will be the envy of the world."

Miss Grenville clapped her hands. "I cannot wait!"

"Pardon the interruption, your grace." Mrs. Epworth, a recent widow, stepped into the conversation. "Can you tell me more about this Society for Creative and Performing Arts? I would love to be a patron."

"Absolutely." Kate grinned back at her.

In no time, the idea had caught on and the partygoers began to tease each other about whether they would attend as sponsors or as performers.

Joy filled Kate's heart. She would spend every moment over the next few weeks continuing to spread the word, but she no longer held any doubts. Her idea was going to work. She could *feel* it. The energy pulsed everywhere around her.

Lady Grenville swooped into Kate's path with a frown. "His grace didn't deign to join us?"

"You know Ravenwood," Lord Grenville said with a laugh before Kate could reply. "Wed to his work, he is."

"Well, now he's wed to his duchess," Lady Grenville insisted petulantly. "One would think he could at least accompany her on her outings."

Kate's cheeks heated at the sound of her earlier unfair thoughts echoed by those around them. She kept her tone casual, but enunciated her reply. "Unlike me, my husband has more important things to do with his time. I'm always well accompanied, however." She nodded toward the refreshment table, where Aunt Havens hovered near a plate of biscuits. "My aunt is the perfect person to attend parties with me."

"A perfect person to be checked into an asylum, you mean," came a nasal sneer from just behind her.

She spun around to find herself face to face with Phineas Mapleton, the *ton*'s most outspoken gossip.

"There is nothing wrong with my Aunt Havens," she snapped.

Mapleton's cruel laugh rang loud. "Nothing except she's been eating off the serving dishes as if the refreshment table were her own private breakfast tray."

Kate jerked her head toward the refreshment table just in time to see Aunt Havens replace a half-eaten biscuit back onto a platter.

"She's *fine*," she managed hotly, before turning and marching through the crowd to rescue the refreshments from her aunt.

Mapleton followed. "She's *old*. You should send her somewhere else to live out her last days."

Kate's eyes stung and she curled her fingers into fists. "She's not going to *die*."

"We'll all die someday," Mapleton corrected with a smirk. "That old biddy is just closer than most."

Kate turned her back on him before she stabbed his eyes out. She hurried over to Aunt Havens. As casually as she could, Kate looped her arm through her aunt's and gently steered her away from the refreshment table.

"Aunt," she said softly. "You can't use serving dishes like plates. Remember?"

Aunt Havens stared at her blankly, her mouth and bodice littered with telltale crumbs.

Kate's throat tightened. "Aunt Havens? Can you hear me?"

"You've lost her," came Mapleton's laughing voice from behind her. "Bats in the belfry."

She tightened her grip on her aunt's hands to keep from

whirling around and leveling him a facer. The Earl of Carlisle had done it once. Kate was willing to pay good money for him to do it again.

"I haven't lost her," she bit out through clenched teeth. Her skin itched with a cold sweat. She would *never* lose Aunt Havens. She couldn't. Swallowing her fear, she bent to her great-aunt's eye level. "Aunt, it's Kate. Do you hear me? Can you see me?"

Aunt Havens blinked and her entire face animated again. "Why are you holding my hands, Kate? This isn't an appropriate venue for us to dance together."

"Oh, that's rich," Mapleton hooted. "Her scolding someone else about proper behavior!"

Aunt Havens frowned. "What on earth is that young man babbling about?"

"Nothing," Kate said quickly. Her heart still beat too quickly from the terror of seeing her aunt unresponsive. "Pay him no mind. He's an imbecile."

"And *she's* nothing more than a great baby," Mapleton shot back. "Do you bathe her and change her, too? She's as helpless and as useless as a child."

Aunt Havens stiffened. "I am not a baby."

"A dog, then." Mapleton's lip curled. "Eating off the serving trays with no more manners than a mutt. You ought not bring her back without a leash. If she's too old for the nursery, you can keep her in the stables."

Kate dragged her away from Mapleton before the blackguard could make any more disparaging comments. She found a private corner behind a painted partition and pulled her aunt out of sight of the crowd.

"We should go, Aunt," she said quietly. "Perhaps you're tired."

"I'm not tired," said Aunt Havens stubbornly. She jerked her arm from Kate's grip. "I'm not a baby. I'm not useless."

"I just..." Kate's heart pounded and she swallowed

hard. "You weren't yourself for a moment, Aunt. I think perhaps you shouldn't be alone. I would hate for something to happen."

Aunt Havens drew herself up tall, her blue eyes shimmering with unshed tears. "Don't patronize me. I am not a danger to myself. And even if I were, I'd rather die as an independent woman than be treated like a child by you."

Kate's chest tightened with guilt. She wrapped her aunt in her arms. "I'm sorry, Aunt. You're right. You're a woman, not a child. I promise never to treat you like one. I swear it."

Only then, finally, did Aunt Havens hug her back.

Chapter Eighteen

Ravenwood was in the east wing listening to his wife explain the provenance of various artifacts she'd used to decorate what had once been an ordinary sitting room into a Greek dayroom when the unmistakable sound of carriage wheels rolled up toward the house.

"Just a moment." He bit back a sigh. He wasn't expecting company or deliveries of any kind, which was why he'd picked this moment to accept Katherine's invitation to view the changes she'd made to her section of the manor. He should've known he would never even have a quarter of an hour free. "Let me see who or what has just arrived."

To his surprise, Katherine pulled a pocket watch from the folds of her skirt. His eyebrows rose. He hadn't known she possessed a watch of any kind. Or pockets.

"It's your cousins," she said once she'd consulted the hour. "Early, I'm afraid."

"My cousins?" He reared back. Now the day was shot completely. He had ledgers to tally... A committee meeting to prepare for...

"Never fear," she assured him. "It's just tea. They're in town for other purposes and will be gone within two hours."

His spirits fell. "I don't have time for tea."

She nodded. "That's why I told them you had meetings

scheduled all day and must send your deepest regrets about being unable to join us."

He stared at her. "I don't even have to greet them?"

"Never again, if that's your desire," she agreed cheerfully. "You hate entertaining people. I love it. This way we both get what we want."

"You *want* to take tea with my cousins?" he repeated, unable to hide his skepticism. The Blaylocks meant well. Some of them, anyway. But even five minutes in their company made him feel like he was drowning.

"I like taking tea with pretty much anyone," she said with a self-deprecating smile. "It will be fun for Aunt Havens, too. We haven't left the house in a fortnight, so it's past time to be a little social."

He frowned. Was that true? He vaguely recalled mention of some Grenville rout a while back, but his nights had been too busy with the House of Lords for him to pay attention to anyone else's schedule.

Parliament was to adjourn in less than a week, which would free up his evenings to spend more time with his wife.

The impending end of the Season also meant far fewer entertainments were to be had… which was why Kate had picked the final week for her opening gala.

His shoulders tightened. He couldn't believe he was just remembering.

"Your event is this week, is it not?" he asked, as if it hadn't just occurred to him. He'd been so busy lately, the best he could do was take each day as it came. He did have the date highlighted in his diary, however. If Katherine believed the success of the evening hinged on his presence at the event, then he would ignore his hatred of crowds and sit there with a smile. He just hoped he didn't have to share a box with his cousins. "Will you be inviting the Blaylocks?"

"Only in town until tomorrow, I'm afraid." The knowing

smile that accompanied her words indicated she'd seen right through the question.

Ravenwood couldn't be disappointed. Once his cousins left, perhaps Katherine could resume the story she'd been telling him about Argonauts and the Golden Fleece. A smile played at his lips. The enthusiasm in her voice indicated she felt as at home among antiquities as he did amongst his flowers. He hoped there would be many more such shared moments in their future.

The butler appeared in the doorway. "Pardon the interruption, your graces. The Blaylock family is in the front parlor."

"Thank you, Simmons. I'll be right there." Katherine waited until the butler left, then touched the tip of her fingers to the back of Ravenwood's hand. "I'll keep them to the front of the house in case you need to visit your garden."

Before he could think of an appropriate response, she swept out into the corridor to go take tea with his family.

He stared after her, stunned.

She wasn't doing him a favor because she—rightly— believed him to be overwhelmed with all his concurrent duties to Parliament and his estate. She was letting him know that it was perfectly fine for him to spend this time doing whatever he wished. Even if that meant nothing more critical than a walk to his garden.

She *understood* him, he realized in surprise. No. More than that. She understood and accepted him precisely how he was.

In a state of some bemusement, he found himself heading not toward his garden, but to his office. He retrieved a key from his inner waistcoat pocket and unlocked the top drawer of his desk.

Once his book of poetry was open before him, he leafed slowly through its pages. He didn't often reread what he had written. The themes were always the same. Hope. Family. Love.

Something had changed over the last few weeks, however. He was no longer writing poetry about a vague hope for a future love, but rather writing poems about someone specific.

His poems were no longer about old dreams. They were about Katherine.

Initially, he hadn't been able to see past her exuberance and chaotic life. But just because it was chaos to him didn't mean it was chaos to her. His heart warmed just thinking about her.

Over the past weeks he'd discovered how surprisingly organized she was. What he'd always assumed was the capricious whim of an idle socialite was actually strategic appearances to boost the success of this event or that.

She was far from the selfish debutante he'd once believed her to be. She opened museums, pioneered support for an artistic community, facilitated fundraising for other people's charities, treated her aunt with more love and caring than he'd ever witnessed anyone display in his life.

Katherine was responsible and driven. Yet she never failed to put family first.

He jerked his head up and stared at his empty office. She *never* failed to put family first.

Family.

Him.

There were a thousand other things she would surely rather be doing than entertain his well-meaning cousins while he took refuge in his office.

He stared at his poetry. All this time, he'd been yearning for a family, yearning for the day when Katherine would want a family—and he already had one. He'd just had to open his eyes.

He shoved his journal back into its drawer and yanked a blank sheet of parchment from a fresh stack.

What Katherine could do that he could not was entertain anyone and everyone with a smile on her face.

What he could do that she could not was pen personal invitations to summon every influential member of the *ton* to Katherine's upcoming gala with the irresistible promise that the reclusive Duke of Ravenwood himself would be present in the front row.

Bring your pocketbook, he underlined in each letter. *I shall match the highest contribution.*

He wrote until his fingers cramped, and then kept going until he had exhausted both his supply of sealing wax and his brain's ability to come up with more names.

Only then did he lean back against his chair and allow his aching hands to relax at his sides.

Even before the feeling had fully returned to his fingers, they were already itching to write something new. Something better. Something for Katherine.

He pulled his journal out of the drawer and opened it to the first blank page.

With trembling hands, he wrote *A Poem For My Wife* across the top.

The words alone sent shivers of fear and excitement along his skin. He had never set out to write a poem about a specific person before. And yet he felt like all his other poems had been practice for this very moment.

He was so focused on choosing every word, on massaging the rhythm, on making every nuance perfect, that at first he didn't even recognize the sound of carriage wheels leaving the property.

His cousins were gone. He could return to Katherine now.

He waited only long enough for the ink to dry before locking his journal away and striding out of his office to find her.

He would ask her to continue showing him the antiques she was so passionate about. And then he would ask her to an early dinner. Even if neither of them were hungry, sharing a glass of wine with her by candlelight would fortify him through the rest of the night with the House of Lords.

Laughter filled the air as he neared the front of the house. He shook his head. What the devil was his wife up to now?

As he entered the main salon, a tiny puff of fur no larger than his fist skidded across the waxed hardwood floor and tumbled head over tail across the tip of his Hessian.

He froze in surprise.

Katherine burst into giggles. "You've met the newest member of our family!"

"Family?" he repeated as the ball of fur attacked his boot as if it had been sent by Napoleon. "What is this?"

"A puppy," she said, all but gurgling with laughter. "Your cousins ended up with more than they could handle, so they were kind enough to leave one here with us."

Kind enough.

He scowled at the creature. Ravenwood House had never had a puppy. He didn't *want* a puppy. If something was going to disrupt their lives, he preferred it to be a child. Someone he could speak with. Read to. Tuck in at night.

"Come here, puppy, puppy," Katherine cooed, dropping to the floor on her knees before his butler, housekeeper, footmen, and an army of maids. She drummed her fingernails against the wood floor. "Puppy, puppy, come over here…"

He stared at her in disbelief. To call this conduct unbefitting a duchess would be the greatest understatement of his life. Any moment now, the beast would piddle on Ravenwood's floor, then run right through it, dirtying the entire parlor.

"Aunt Havens, you try," she called out. "You've always been clever at this. Maybe he'll come to you."

To Ravenwood's utter stupefaction, the elderly Mrs. Havens dropped to all fours with the agility of a ten-year-old boy and wriggled her derrière in the air.

Much like the puppy itself was doing.

With a joyful bark, the creature leapt over Ravenwood's boot and launched itself directly at Mrs. Havens.

The servants were nearly weeping with laughter as they watched the little beast yip and leap and sink its teeth into the exposed hem of Mrs. Havens' petticoat.

"Join us," Katherine called up to him, patting the floor beside her as if Ravenwood, too, was a brainless puppy that would come when called.

To their credit, the staff's laughter dried up into choked horror as they realized not only would the Duke of Ravenwood *not* be rolling about the floor with a scrap of fluff, but soon neither would his duchess.

"Aunt Havens, you're the *best*." Katherine clapped her hands, her husband—and their entire watching staff—once again forgotten. "How do I make him come to me?" She glanced up at Ravenwood, her eyes sparkling. "Can you do it?"

He stared at her as coldly as he could, hoping she would understand without the need for public chastisement that as Duke and Duchess of Ravenwood, their duty was to uphold propriety at all times. Not to scamper on floors with puppies.

She gazed back at him with happy, unwavering exuberance, obviously certain that at any moment he, too, would throw himself to his knees and begin cooing like a lunatic.

The worst part of it was…he rather wanted to.

Not only was the puppy adorable, Katherine was almost irresistible. She enjoyed everything she did so thoroughly, loved everyone and everything so unconditionally, smiled at him with so much wholehearted joy…

But he was duke.

No matter how much he might wish he could join her, his conduct and bearing affected more than just his reputation. His every action reflected back onto the dukedom itself. Yet he realized that wasn't what she wanted.

If he allowed her to chip away at his armor so that he became closer to her, he could lose respect in the eyes of everyone else.

Both paths risked something he dared not lose. But only one path was the right one. The proper one.

"I've decided to name him Francis," she said hesitantly, her smile finally starting to wobble. "M-may we keep him?"

"No," he said flatly. He leaned over and scooped the little beast up into his hands. "He looks more like a Jasper."

He threw himself to the floor between his wife and Mrs. Havens and let the puppy gnaw a hole in his waistcoat.

Chapter Nineteen

It wasn't until Ravenwood had worked through luncheon without a single interruption that he realized there hadn't *been* any interruptions for weeks.

The maids were still cleaning his office—there was not so much as a speck of dust upon any surface—but he had not actually glimpsed a single mobcap.

He crossed to the bell pull and gave the sharp double-tug that indicated he wished a quick tray of easy-to-consume-at-one's-desk food to be brought to his office. Yet he did not immediately return to his chair.

Yesterday, when the arrival of his cousins had interrupted Katherine's explanation of the items in her Egyptian salon, he had been shocked to realize an entire fortnight had passed since he'd last had the opportunity to converse with her.

'Twas now occurring to him that they wouldn't even have had those brief moments, had he not finally taken her up on her invitation to visit her in her half of Ravenwood House.

Parliament was the culprit. The House of Lords, the blasted Coinage Committee. Meetings, missives, drafting bills. Everyone needed something from him every second of the day. He was constantly tugged in a thousand different directions.

Except by his wife.

What had she been doing in the weeks between the Grenville soirée and his cousins' noon visit? He assumed working on her arts society or waltzing in the parlor with his butler, but the truth was, Ravenwood had absolutely no idea.

The door eased open and a footman stepped in bearing a silver tray. "Your meal, your grace."

Ravenwood motioned toward his desk.

The footman set down the tray and moved silently back toward the door.

Ravenwood retook his seat, then paused. "John?"

The footman turned toward him. "Yes, your grace?"

"Where are the maids assigned to this corridor? I haven't seen them in weeks."

"Yes, your grace." The footman cleared his throat. "Her grace rescheduled all the staff covering your office to work evenings instead of days, so as not to bother you while you are working. The same responsibilities are being accomplished. They're simply being handled while you are away from your desk."

Ravenwood swallowed. How incredibly...*thoughtful*.

Katherine had gone well out of her way to ensure he had all the uninterrupted privacy he desired for his duties and his poetry.

It had worked so well that Ravenwood hadn't even noticed. Hadn't thanked her when he'd had the chance.

Hadn't even carved out a full hour of his time to give her in return.

"Where is her grace now?" he asked the footman.

John shook his head. "Can't rightly say, your grace. When she's not studying Lady Amelia's journals, she's usually shadowing one of the staff and taking notes." He lifted a shoulder. "Can't imagine what she finds to put in her journals that Lady Amelia hadn't already written in hers."

Ravenwood stared at him. "Her grace what? She has

Lady Amelia's old journals? There must be dozens of them."

"Sixty-two," the footman agreed. "We carried them up."

Ravenwood shook his head. "Why would she want them?"

"She's memorizing them," the footman explained. "Each shift takes turns quizzing her from the volumes pertaining to our duties. Her grace is a right quick study," he added with obvious pride. "Memorized the ones pertaining to this corridor in her very first week."

Ravenwood's mouth fell open. "I can understand her grace wishing to acquaint herself with the management of this estate, but my sister's extensive journals were an obsession, not a requirement. Why would my wife wish to read them, much less memorize them?"

"Because Lady Amelia has everything memorized," the footman answered simply. "Everyone knows she was a stupendous mistress—you've said so on many occasions yourself. Her grace believes she must do the same in order to be the kind of mistress you desire."

"I don't need her to be my *sister*," Ravenwood spluttered.

The footman stared at him blankly. "You didn't tell her grace to send for the journals?"

"I did not." Ravenwood ran an unsteady hand through his hair as guilt assailed him.

Of course he hadn't told her to send for the journals. He hadn't told her anything.

He hadn't even seen her.

While he'd been slaving over parliamentary duties...or writing poetry...or relaxing in his garden, Katherine had been killing herself to learn every aspect of his estate.

Simply because she wished to please him. To be a duchess he could be proud of.

His throat grew thick.

Whenever he got overwhelmed or needed a break, he

simply left his office.

Kate's office, on the other hand, was every inch and every corner of Ravenwood House.

There wasn't a single room to escape to that didn't have pending duties, corresponding journal entries, servants, history, details and schedules she would feel expected to know and manage and memorize.

He had spent the past fortnight irritated with his useless compatriots in the House of Lords.

She had spent hers trying to be someone she was not.

He had been wrong about marriage turning his world upside down. The compromise hadn't disrupted his life one whit.

It had only upended hers.

"John," he said, pushing to his feet. "I've changed my mind. Please return this tray to the kitchen, and have them prepare a picnic instead. I will take it by the front door."

The footman retrieved the silver tray without question and disappeared down the hall.

Ravenwood stepped out of his office and closed the door firmly behind him. He was not the only one in need of an occasional visit to a private sanctuary.

Katherine didn't even have one.

He strode from the west wing to the east wing in search of her. She was not in her chambers or in her parlor. He did, however, find Mrs. Havens in her guest quarters, playing with the puppy.

He sketched a bow. "Where is Katherine?"

Mrs. Havens glanced at the clock on her mantel. "Half past two. She must be on her way to the laundry. Today is ironing day for bedlinen."

Ravenwood rubbed his nose. From the sound of it, even Mrs. Havens had read those cursed journals.

"Bring Jasper," he ordered and spun back toward the corridor. "We're going to find her."

Mrs. Havens scooped the puppy into a basket and

hurried after him. "Why? Did something happen?"

"Something is about to happen." He led the way to the laundry. "This family is going on a picnic. Right. Now."

He found Katherine before a roaring fire, hauling an iron from the flames with a large hooked stick.

"*Duchess*," he barked, his chest tightening at the sight. "Please step away from the laundry."

She leapt back, startled. It was impossible to say whether the flush on her cheeks was due to his unexpected arrival or the infernal heat from the blaze.

He took her arm and all but yanked her to safety.

His first impulse was to yell at her. To shake her. To tell her never again was she to be leaning so close to a fire that the puffed sleeves of her linen day dress still carried the scent of smoke.

The purple smudges beneath her eyes stopped him.

If she spent every shift immersing herself in the inner workings of Ravenwood House, when on earth did she sleep?

She *wasn't* sleeping, he realized. She was working harder than any of his servants. Harder than he himself. She was spending every hour of every day here in the trenches or up memorizing journals.

For him.

He kissed her. Right there in front of the laundry maids, in front of Mrs. Havens and the puppy, out in the open where anyone might see. He kissed her because he needed to. Because he needed *her*.

And then he dragged her to the front door so he could pick up their picnic basket.

"What are we doing?" she stammered as he towed her out the door. "Where are we going?"

He fished the brass key from his pocket and placed it into her hand. "To my garden. *Our* garden. We're having a picnic."

A smile brightened her tired eyes. "I love picnics."

He swung her into his arms and carried her the rest of the way, ignoring the bang of the picnic basket against his side as he walked.

She was tired, he told himself. Carrying her was practical. Snuggling her close so he could press frequent kisses to her hair, her nose, her forehead…

He did it again just because he could. Because he liked to kiss her. Liked how she felt in his arms. Liked that she carried the key to his garden. And the key to his heart.

Only when they reached the gate did he set her back on her feet.

Katherine slid the key into the lock and grinned over her shoulder at Mrs. Havens. "You're going to love this, Aunt."

Mrs. Havens gasped in delight as the gate swung open to reveal his wild, colorful paradise.

Ravenwood set down the picnic basket and tried not to look too pleased.

This time, he hadn't been nervous about showing it to someone new. He hadn't even thought about it. Bringing his family here simply felt right.

He opened the basket and shook out a large blanket for the three of them to sit on.

Jasper had already discovered a butterfly amongst the cherry trees, and was merrily bounding about the tall grass and sea of flowers to give chase.

"Have you had luncheon?" Ravenwood asked as he prepared a plate.

Katherine's blank expression indicated she had not.

He filled the plate even higher before handing it to her. "Eat."

"Thank you," she said, but waited until he and Mrs. Havens also had plates before turning to hers.

He was famished. Bread and cheese had never tasted so good in his life. The wine and fruit were like ambrosia.

He was happy to see his wife also eating with pleasure, but angry with himself for making her feel like the only way she could be appreciated was to enslave herself to the perfect management of his household.

"No more memorizing," he ordered.

She blinked at him. "What?"

"My sister was an excellent mistress to Ravenwood House. She's also barmy for memory pantries and cross-referenced guest lists. You do not need to be Lady Amelia. I don't *want* you to be Lady Amelia. I want you to be Katherine." He took her hand and brought it to his lips. "That's who I married."

She shook her head. "You married a hoyden, not a duchess. I'm not what you wanted or needed. But I'm trying my best to—"

"Sweetheart." He touched his hand to her face. "I like you just as you are. You don't need to become anyone else for me to be proud of you."

Her eyes widened and shimmered. She blinked rapidly, then threw herself into his arms.

He lay his cheek atop her head and held on tight.

She was only partially right. When they'd first been compromised, neither had been what the other wanted. But she was definitely what he needed.

He had married the right woman after all.

Chapter Twenty

Kate sat on the floor of her great-aunt's sitting room thanking the heavens for Jasper the puppy.

He was the one thing helping to keep her mind off everything that could go wrong or right at tomorrow's inauguration of the London Society of the Creative and Performing Arts.

Aunt Havens was in a wingback chair, hunched over a scrap of embroidery that she still refused to let anyone see. Such spells had been happening more and more often.

Ravenwood was with the House of Lords. As usual. But not only did Parliament adjourn next week, there was no meeting tomorrow. Her husband would be free for the entire evening, as would all of the other peers making up the House of Lords.

Kate hadn't been able to promote the event as much as she would have liked, for fear of an uncomfortable incident with Aunt Havens.

She wasn't willing to risk her aunt getting into trouble or danger, nor was she willing to risk subjecting her aunt to the level of humiliation she'd suffered as the brunt of Phineas Mapleton's cruel comments.

So she'd stayed in. And concentrated on being mistress of Ravenwood House.

Nonetheless, a steady stream of missives had flooded her escritoire, letting Kate know that this earl and that baroness were delighted to attend her event, and intended to ensure their financial contribution would be the largest.

It was baffling. Terrifying. Exhilarating.

She thrummed with so much nervous excitement, she could barely sit still, let alone eat or sleep.

"Your grace?"

Kate lifted her head up from the puppy to see the butler and a gaggle of footmen clustered in the doorway. "Yes, Simmons?"

"Several large crates have just arrived for you." He cleared his throat. "The calling card merely reads, 'Repeating history.'"

He held out the card, but Kate had no need to see it. She was already on her feet, handing Jasper off to Aunt Havens. *Repeating history* could only mean one thing.

The furniture had arrived!

"Take everything to the back parlor. The one with the Ravenwood family portrait."

The butler blinked as if he did not quite comprehend her orders. "Your grace?"

"It's not Egyptian artifacts, Simmons. I swear." She grinned at him and clasped her hands to her chest.

This was perfect. This was better than perfect. It was not only exactly what she needed to distract her mind from tomorrow's inaugural gala, it was perfect timing for Ravenwood as well. He had mentioned he thought he might be able to make it home early. Perhaps she could reveal her surprise to him this very night!

She raced to the parlor in order to direct the footmen as to where to put which piece.

As it turned out, no such direction was necessary. Not only was a visual map staring back at them from the painting, the butler had served long enough to remember the room as it was twenty years ago and needed no instruction on arranging each item.

Once the staff realized what was inside the crates, their enthusiasm matched Kate's own. They marveled at the uncanny resemblance of the new pieces to the old painting. Simmons' only complaint was that if anything, the replacement furniture was in better condition than the originals.

Kate hugged herself. She couldn't wait to see Ravenwood's expression when he saw the reconstruction. He would see how much she cared. How hard she was trying to know *him*. To make him happy.

"When is the last time my husband came by this room?" she asked the footmen.

They glanced at each other uncomfortably. "Not since the day you took down your Egyptian things."

Her spirits fell a little. She had pictured him visiting the parlor every night. Imagined herself incredibly clever for having slipped the painting out for an entire day without him noticing. When in fact, he might not visit again unless she dragged him here by the hand.

"Is that usual?" she asked the butler. "Has he always avoided this parlor?"

Simmons shook his head. "The longest he ever went between visits was a few days at the most."

She frowned. "Then why hasn't he been by for weeks?"

The butler's smile was kind. "He gave the east wing to you."

She blinked rapidly. Foolish man. But not as big a fool as herself, for not realizing how much he was giving up when he'd proclaimed the east wing as hers.

Well, she was about to give it back.

"In that case, please don't tell him what we've done." She gave the staff a conspiratorial grin. "Now that I know he won't see the room until I show him, I'd like to pick the perfect moment. Next week, I think, when Parliament has adjourned and we have more time for each other."

The footmen nodded and promised not to spill a word. Simmons complimented her on the fine work, and assured her his grace would love every inch of it.

Kate smiled back. She no longer wanted Ravenwood to love the furniture. She wanted him to love *her*.

As she walked back to her aunt's sitting room, Kate's mind hummed with thoughts of how her future with Ravenwood might be. Which led to thoughts of what the future might bring in general.

Which led to thoughts of Aunt Havens.

She was fine for right now—*mostly* fine, anyway—but Kate needed to keep her safe when she wouldn't be able to be by her side.

Ravenwood, she remembered suddenly.

Warmth spread through her. She was no longer in this alone. Her spirits lightened. Gone were the days of Kate and Aunt Havens against the world. Now there were three of them. Ravenwood would keep everyone safe.

She reentered her aunt's sitting room just in time to see Aunt Havens swat Jasper out of her embroidery basket.

"Beastly creature," she muttered with a comical eye roll toward Kate. "Can't he see I'm working?"

Kate scooped the adorable beast into her arms and stretched out on the chaise longue. "What are you working on?"

"A gift for you."

Kate sat up, intrigued. "What is it?"

Aunt Havens hid the basket from view. "Something for you to remember me by. I think you'll love it."

Kate's heart skipped a beat as the blood drained from her face. "I don't need a gewgaw to remember you by. Don't *say* things like that."

"Memories are good things, not bad things, Kate." Aunt Havens smiled. "Just think of all the memories you're making with your husband. Isn't life so much richer with love in it?"

"My life is richer with both of you in it." Kate pushed stiffly to her feet, leaving Jasper to look after her aunt. "I'm going to my room to begin preparing for tomorrow. When you decide to stop talking nonsense, knock on my door."

Chapter Twenty-One

Kate's eyes refused to focus on her wardrobe. She was too afraid. Her heart seized up every time she considered the possibility of losing Aunt Havens.

Of course she knew her aunt would die someday. Everybody eventually died. But there was no reason to prepare for death *now*. Not today, not this year, not anytime soon.

Aunt Havens might get confused sometimes, but she was otherwise in the peak of health. More fragile than before? Perhaps. Too thin? Possibly. But no one was asking her to scale a mountain. Her days were filled with nothing more strenuous than petting a puppy and embroidering squares of linen.

As long as she stayed here at home, took her meals with Kate, and spent her time relaxing—there was no reason to think there weren't many happy years ahead of them. Decades, even.

Aunt Havens had cared for Kate her entire life, and now it was Kate's turn to keep Aunt Havens safe.

When at last the knock came on Kate's door, she sagged with relief. Aunt Havens had abandoned her funereal line of thought and had decided to help Kate select her wardrobe for tomorrow's event after all.

Except the knock hadn't come from the corridor, but

rather the connecting door leading to her husband's bedchamber.

A glance at the clock on the mantel indicated it was far too early for Ravenwood to be home from Parliament, but why on earth would his valet be begging entrance at this hour? Or—God forbid—Aunt Havens hadn't come to patch things up and accidentally wandered into the wrong bedchamber, had she?

Heart in her throat, Kate flung the door open wide.

Broad shoulders, a mop of chestnut curls, and clear green eyes met her gaze.

"Ravenwood?" she choked out in surprise, a half-hysterical laugh wheezing from her lungs.

He lifted a brow. "You were expecting someone else?"

She threw herself into his arms and wrapped her arms about him tight.

Yes. Yes, she had been expecting someone else. Yes, her aunt was becoming so erratic that for a moment, she had truly believed her aunt had entered the wrong bedchamber and was trying to find her way out.

Kate buried her face in his chest, but the words would not come. They hurt too much. Scared her too deeply. She didn't wish to talk about her aunt's fickle sanity. She didn't want to think about what it might mean.

She just wanted to forget. To feel better. To let someone else be in charge.

Ravenwood was safe. His arms were safe. Warm, strong, dependable. He had never let anyone down in his life. He was the one person she could rely on without fail.

She hugged him tighter.

"What happened?" he asked as he stroked her hair.

"Aunt Havens," Kate mumbled against his cravat.

He tilted her face toward his, frowning. "Is she all right?"

"*Yes*," she said fiercely. "But she acts like she's going to die."

Ravenwood made no answer.

Kate appreciated his reserve. She didn't need to be told the obvious—that someday it would happen. That it would hurt deeply. That she would never truly get over it.

Ravenwood understood. He would not be a duke today if he too had not experienced loss. He knew better than to fill the silence with platitudes about *enjoy the moments you have* or *she'll go to a better place*. Those things were true, but right now they gave no comfort.

Only his warm, steady embrace brought comfort.

"You're home early," she murmured into his chest.

"You're up late," he countered softly. "'Twas the first time I returned from Parliament and saw light still flickering beneath the door. Are you tired? Do you want to sleep?"

"Yes. No." She gave a hiccupy laugh at her own muddled thoughts. "I don't know."

He scooped her up in his arms and carried her to her bed.

She was already in her nightrail. She'd gone ahead and prepared for bed once she'd realized her mind was incapable of focusing on tomorrow. She hadn't climbed into bed, however, because she had been hoping for a knock at the door.

Now that he had arrived, she wasn't certain she was ready to be left alone. But he was a busy man. He hadn't yet had a chance to unwind from his exhausting parliamentary session.

She knew what a toll being around so many people took on him. To recover, he needed privacy. Not a wife plagued by fears of an eventuality that could still be many years away. She would not be offended if he bid her goodnight and retreated to his own chamber.

He tucked her into bed, then sat in the closest chair to begin tugging off his boots.

She held her breath as he removed his gloves, his overcoat, his waistcoat, and piled each neatly folded item on the cushion of an empty chair.

When he was clad in nothing more than soft calfskin breeches and the billowing white lawn of his undershirt, he slid beneath the sheets of her bed and pulled her back into his arms.

She clutched him tight.

He kissed the top of her head and just held her.

"Aunt Havens thinks she's going to die," she whispered after her heart had calmed. "She's making a token for me to remember her by."

He brushed stray tendrils from her face. "You don't need a token."

She shook her head. Not now, now ever. Aunt Havens was unforgettable.

He stroked his thumb against her cheek. "Perhaps she isn't expecting to die anytime soon, but wishes to create some sort of keepsake while she's healthy and still can. Think about your artists. Painters paint portraits they hope will live on, without specifically thinking about their mortality. They just want to create."

"Yes," she decided firmly. He was right. "That's all it was. She's trying to be practical."

Which proved that Aunt Havens' mind *was* still sound. Only a sane person planned for contingencies and concerned herself with mundane practical matters. There was nothing at all for Kate to get in such a tizzy over. She nestled closer into Ravenwood's arms.

"You're the bravest person I know," he told her softly.

Her? She lifted her head in surprise. "In what way?"

"You don't hesitate to open your heart." He cupped her cheek, his eyes dark. "For some people, that is the most frightening risk of all."

She scoffed at the absurd notion. "I'm not brave. I'm a coward. In case you hadn't noticed, I'm terrified of being alone."

His eyes met hers in silence.

"Don't leave me," she whispered.

"I won't." His mouth covered hers.

He pulled her close. His kisses weren't tentative. They were demanding, urgent. In his arms, she wasn't just safe. She was *alive*. Every fiber of her being was attuned to the heat of his skin, the hard planes of his muscles, the eagerness coursing through her veins. Everything she needed.

She met each kiss with passion. Her body still remembered the delicious, foreign sensation of his strong fingers against her bare skin and she longed for him to do it again. She tangled her fingers in his hair and pressed herself against him.

He was strength and power. Gentle and resilient. He was so much bigger, so solid and commanding, that she couldn't help but give herself to him completely.

When his hand cupped her breast, she arched into his touch. She craved this, craved him. His fingers found her straining nipple. Tugged. Teased. A sharp longing began between her legs, building with every pinch of his fingers, every lick of his tongue against hers.

Her head fell back. With him, she felt more than mere comfort. She felt desired. Every kiss told her how badly he wanted her. She was important. She was his.

He yanked up the hem of her nightrail. She parted her legs. She *was* his. Her body throbbed with anticipation.

She wanted him to take his time. She wanted him to hurry. She wanted—

He lowered his mouth to her breast just as he dipped a finger into the slick heat between her legs.

She gasped at the unexpected pleasure of the twin sensations. Her muscles tightened as she arched into him. Her mind could no longer process anything except the sensual pressure building inside her. She gripped his shoulders as if to let go would mean falling into an abyss and he was the only one who could save her.

Perhaps he *was* the only one who could save her. She had never felt so valuable, so treasured as she did with him.

A moan escaped her lips as his thumb rubbed against a sensitive spot at the apex between her legs. Her body thrummed with coiled desire. She didn't want his wicked fingers anymore. She wanted *him*. Her husband.

The French letters.

Frustration ripped through her as she realized it was long past the moment to start soaking protective sheaths in water. He was here now. Her body was *ready* now.

This was the moment to show him how deeply she longed to connect with him and how much he meant to her. He had accepted her. All of her. He had not only given her a home, but made her feel it. Home was more than a house. It was his arms, his garden, their bed.

Their future.

She had decided weeks ago that there was no possible way she could ever let Ravenwood go. The bigger question was ensuring he had no reason to let *her* go.

He desired her. That much was clear. They were good together, even out of the bedroom. He'd proven that in his garden, time and again. He wanted her.

He also wanted a family.

The idea of losing a child still terrified her. It likely always would. But she no longer equated the thought with loneliness and regret.

She had Ravenwood now. As long as they were together, she would never be lonely. Her biggest regret would be walking away. Not having his child. Not building a family.

This was the first time he had come to her bedchamber since their failed wedding night. She was bared to him. Open to his touch. To pleasure.

If she stopped him again, how long would it be until he came back? Did she even wish to stop him? She moaned. Her body certainly didn't. Her hips rose to meet him with every thrust of his finger.

She shoved both hands to his waist, yanking up his shirt, tugging at the fall of his breeches. She wanted all of him, right now. She wanted to give him all of herself.

He flung his shirt over his head and unbuttoned his fall.

She reached for him.

If a child came from this union, it would not be a nightmare, but a miracle. A gift. A baby would be part of themselves. Someone they both would love. Someone utterly worth the risk.

A shiver danced over her skin as the hard length of his member nudged against her aching core. She belonged here. She belonged with him.

He belonged inside her.

She gasped and tightened her grip on his hair as he eased between her legs. He was too big, too hard, but as soon as his finger returned to her sensitive nub, everything fell away.

All she could feel was pleasure.

She wrapped her legs about his hips. Pressure built as their bodies merged together. Every surge, every thrust, not only brought her closer to him but also made her feel part of something bigger. With him, she was more than merely Kate.

She was complete.

Chapter Twenty-Two

Ravenwood awoke with his forearm muscles tingling. He'd fallen asleep with his arms about his wife, and they'd slept the night wrapped in each other's embrace.

He slid out of bed as carefully as he could without waking her and set about collecting his discarded clothing.

While it was unusual, perhaps, for a duke to spend the entirety of the night in his duchess's bedchamber, he did not believe the practice to indicate a lack of propriety on the part of the husband—and he didn't care a flying fig if it did.

As far as he was concerned, sharing a bed with his wife was about to become his favorite custom.

He felt himself smiling as he bathed, dressed, and prepared for the day. He felt like his entire body was smiling, inside and out.

Katherine had that sort of effect on him.

His step lighter than it had been in years, he made his way to his office. His thoughts, however, were still with Katherine.

He'd meant what he had said about her being brave. She opened her heart and loved completely and unconditionally, without reservation. Unlike him, she didn't hold back when she feared the possibility of getting hurt.

He shouldn't either. Not with her. Not when they were

so close to having the sort of marriage, the sort of connection he'd always dreamed of having.

If he wanted that kind of life, then he had to risk opening his heart to get it.

Oh, who was he fooling? She'd been in his heart for some time. He sat down at his desk and unlocked the drawer that contained his poetry.

Slowly, he paged through the words he'd written since Katherine had turned his world upside down.

It hadn't happened overnight, but the truth was as apparent to him on the page as it was in his heart. He'd fallen in love. Wholly, hopelessly, irrevocably. Every word on every page declared the truth.

He wondered what she might say if she knew he'd written such wistful, lovesick verses about her.

The memory of her dismissal of people like him as fools pretending to be Lord Byron made his ears burn with shame. He knew what she'd say. He slammed the book closed and locked it back in its drawer.

Perhaps someday he might risk showing her one of his poems. Years from now. When he was certain she loved him unconditionally.

He forced himself to turn to his ledgers. There was no House of Lords meeting tonight, but the Coinage Committee was scheduled to present their final recommendations tomorrow. He would ring for a breakfast tray and spend the entire day finalizing his portion of the report in order to keep his mind free from parliamentary duties.

Tonight was about Katherine.

He was so proud of her. Not just for daring to dream, but daring to accomplish her dreams. It wasn't that she believed failure wasn't an option. All that mattered to her was that she tried. And because of her optimism and perseverance, every time she tried—she succeeded.

The House of Lords could use a few more like her.

Ugh. Ravenwood rubbed his face. The blasted Coinage

Committee.

Over the course of the next several hours, he worked without cease. He penned the final flourishes on the report he'd spent the past month on just as the light in his windows began to fade dramatically.

Dark clouds rolled over the fading sunset. If the black horizon was any indication, it was going to rain all night long. He glanced at the clock on the mantel. Seven o'clock.

It was time to get ready for tonight's performance.

He pushed to his feet just as his butler entered the room bearing a sealed missive on a silver platter.

"Pardon the interruption, your grace. An urgent message has arrived. A footman is waiting below to run your response back to his master."

Ravenwood's stomach sank as he recognized Lord Montague's seal. The marquess was the only other member of the Coinage Committee with any brains. An importunate message at this time at night could not presage anything good.

He lifted the folded parchment from the silver tray and sliced open the wax. With trepidation, he began to read.

No.

His eyes fluttered closed and he curled his fingers into fists. The other half-dozen imbeciles comprising the Coinage Committee had decided to eschew Ravenwood's clearheaded logic, and were instead at White's gentleman's club on St. James Street, attempting to sway the vote before it even happened.

They wanted to ignore the dismal slope of the post-war economy and cast all coinage in gold, and in larger sizes. They thought a nation rich enough to do so would raise England's prestige in the eyes of all competing nations. They even considered pennies with the faces of their peers.

Montague and Ravenwood recognized such twaddle for the poppycock it was. What England needed was to stabilize its currency, not to unbalance it further.

They should be reintroducing silver, not hemorrhaging gold. They needed to define a predictable value for the pound sterling. Anything they could to curb its disquieting devaluation.

The *ton*, however, liked sparkle more than they liked logic. Who wouldn't wish to see his profile silhouetted in gold?

Idiots, all of them. If such a foolish idea gained wings, the House would pass the motion with a near unanimous vote.

Ravenwood could not let that happen.

By himself, Lord Montague would not be able to stem the tide. The gold fanatics would poison the ears of anyone within reach and tomorrow they would disregard all of his month-long research as being capricious and irrelevant. All anyone would care about was the chance to see their face reflected back at them.

However, if Ravenwood could make an appearance at White's *right now*, evidence in hand, he and Montague might be able to sway opinion for a few of the brightest minds and still manage to salvage a responsible fiscal program for the Crown to carry out over the following year.

Ravenwood threw the wadded up missive into the fireplace. "Summon my coach, Simmons."

The butler hesitated. "My apologies, your grace. I had told them you wouldn't need it for an hour. I'll hurry and—"

"Leave that coach for my wife as scheduled," Ravenwood interrupted with a sigh. "Send up the landau. I have an errand."

Simmons' eyes widened. "Shall I tell her grace you'll meet her at the gala?"

Ravenwood set his icy ducal mask back in place to hide his regret. "I will not be attending the gala. I will be at White's handling a parliamentary issue. One's first duty must always be to one's country."

Simmons was far too well bred to so much as frown at the discovery his master would not be attending the duchess's grand event, but the flicker of censure in his eyes matched the hollowness in Ravenwood's stomach.

Yes, he well knew his duty to his country. But what about his duty to Katherine?

"Well?" he prompted.

Simmons flinched. "Yes, your grace. Summoning the landau this very moment."

As his butler turned toward the door, Ravenwood couldn't stop himself from asking, "Where is my wife now?"

Simmons paused. "Strolling the grounds, your grace. She says it helps to ease her nerves."

Ravenwood nodded curtly.

Of course even his indomitable wife would be vulnerable to the occasional bout of nervousness. She was human.

She was also expecting her husband to lend his support and comfort.

He ran a hand through his hair. Damn those fools. He *had* to go stop this nonsense. Even if it took all night.

If the Coinage Committee managed to bollocks up the economy even worse than it was currently headed, all of England would suffer for it—including Katherine. He could not allow that to happen.

Nor could he allow her to think he wasn't present because he didn't care.

He hesitated for a mere heartbeat before unlocking his desk drawer and withdrawing his secret book of poetry. No matter how nervous Katherine was about the success of tonight's gala, it couldn't come close to the terror Ravenwood felt at showing her a single word from the journal's pages.

It would mean exposing himself completely. A vein, laid bare. His heart in her hands.

He took a deep, shuddering breath and strode forcefully

through the door.

Katherine was worth it.

Chapter Twenty-Three

A crack of thunder growled through the darkening heavens.

Kate reached out to loop her arm through Aunt Havens'. The sky had been clear when they'd set out to distract Kate from nervousness about tonight's inaugural event but in the space of a quarter hour, a black storm rose over the horizon to rapidly swallow the sky.

The return walk was taking thrice as long as it ought, and the dropping temperature boded ill for her aunt's elderly constitution.

"We should make haste," she murmured without altering her pace. At Aunt Havens' age, hurrying could lead to a fall. And a fall could mean grave injury. "Take my hand."

Aunt Havens scowled. "You promised you wouldn't treat me like a child."

Kate kept her feet moving along the path. "You're not a child. You're my aunt and my dearest friend. Which is why I wouldn't want you somewhere you wouldn't be safe or have a good time."

Aunt Havens' lip quivered. "You don't want me at your opening gala?"

"You *must* attend tonight's gala," Kate said patiently. "You're the other half of my heart. Seeing you and

Ravenwood in the front row will give me the strength I need not to lose my mind completely. But Ravenwood won't be there next month, or the month after. He loathes making public appearances and I won't force him to do something he hates."

"But I love being social," Aunt Havens protested, her thin fingers gripping Kate's arm. "I love everything you do. I don't want to miss any of it."

"I'm not leaving you somewhere to fend for yourself," Kate said, her voice flat. Phineas Mapleton wasn't the only bully in the *beau monde*. And a theatre's many nooks and crannies held far more opportunities for trouble than a mere refreshment table. "Be reasonable, aunt. I won't be able to be at your side."

Aunt Havens' eyes flashed. "I don't need a nursemaid. I'm a grown woman. Nothing would happen."

Kate sighed. If only she could be certain that were true.

The problem—or the blessing—was that her aunt had been refreshingly normal ever since the Grenville soiree. Oh, certainly, there had been scattered moments of temporary confusion or wandering of the corridors, mostly at nighttime, but for a full fortnight, Aunt Havens had been Aunt Havens. Caring, clearheaded, and delightful.

It made Kate look like a peevish goose-cap to suggest her aunt incapable of occupying a theater seat without supervision. It made Kate *feel* like a peevish goose-cap. What if she was overreacting, and Aunt Havens would be perfectly fine?

Then again…what if she would not?

"It's not that you need a nursemaid," she told her aunt. "It's that I will be going mad with all the preparations and timing and the myriad things that can go awry with the performances at any moment. I won't even be able to stop and talk to you."

Aunt Havens' chin trembled. "You won't have to talk to me. I already know you're going to succeed beyond anyone's imaginings, including your own. I want to be there to see it happen. I want to cheer you on."

Kate took a deep breath. That was her dream, too. "Let's hurry inside. We need to leave for the theater in less than an hour and neither of us is ready. Right now everything seems overwhelming. I spent all afternoon hunting for my best evening gloves and I still haven't found them."

"Ohh," Aunt Havens said with a chuckle. "I took them days ago."

Kate's mouth dropped open in disbelief. That completely unlike her. "You snuck into my bedchamber and nicked my best evening gloves?"

Aunt Havens nodded. "I needed them."

"You—Aunt, give them back," Kate spluttered. Her aunt's moments of confusion were obviously worse than she'd thought. "As soon as we get into the house."

"No." Aunt Havens set her chin mutinously.

Kate stiffened her spine. There was no sense arguing with someone who could not think logically. If she wished to wear gloves, she would simply have to wear a pair of ill-fitting ones from last year, or else a more comfortable pair that weren't quite fine enough for the occasion.

"*This*, Aunt," she said in mounting irritation. "This is why you can't be left alone in a crowded theatre. You'll eat from the serving trays, steal people's evening gloves… How am I supposed to concentrate on managing dozens of performers when all I can do is worry about you?"

"How can you leave me behind?" A tremor shook Aunt Havens' voice and she yanked her arm free from Kate's. "I know I'm getting older. That's why I don't want to miss a single one of your achievements. Every day, I think: what if this is the last time I'm able?"

Kate's throat seized up, preventing her from responding. What if tonight *was* the last time Aunt Havens attended one of Kate's events?

Aunt Havens jerked away from Kate and marched up the

final walkway to the entrance of Ravenwood House by herself.

Kate stood in the front lawn and watched her go.

The first droplets of rain fell from the clouds above, splattering on Kate's nose with icy wetness. Yet she no longer felt like rushing inside to don her favorite evening gown. All she wanted to do was throw herself into her aunt's arms and hold on tight.

The front door swung open and her husband stepped outside.

Warmth spread through Kate's chest and her shoulders started to relax. Ravenwood was strong. He made everything better. Tonight, he would stay by Aunt Havens' side. Tomorrow, they would figure out a compromise for the future. Something that would make all three of them happy.

Ravenwood sprinted forward, opening a large black umbrella as he ran. He held it over her head and kissed her. "Haven't you the sense to come in out of the rain? I cannot have you catching cold before you even leave the house."

She wrapped her arms about him and laid her cheek against his warm chest. He was her rock. She couldn't help but love him.

When they'd first been compromised, she'd believed him a soulless blueblood with a heart of ice. How wrong she had been. He was business and order and beauty and wildness all wrapped into one. He wasn't just perfect—he was perfect for her.

He pressed a kiss to her forehead. "How are you feeling?"

"Terrified," she answered honestly. "My grand inaugural event is only 'inaugural' if it takes off and more events follow. No one I've spoken to truly believes it will. The *ton* acts like it's a one-time charity event. The performers are convinced there will never be a second show. I *know* a society like this would be wonderful for our city. But everything hinges on everything else, and the slightest disruption could derail the whole scheme."

He stared at her, his green eyes unfathomable.

She tried to smile. "At least two things will go right tonight. I'll have my two favorite people seated in the front row. I'll glance down at you any time I get frightened and I'll be able to regain my strength."

"I…" Ravenwood loosened her arms from about his waist so he could retrieve a journal from inside his greatcoat. "I have something for you."

Carriage wheels crunched along wet gravel and she jerked her gaze around his shoulder in surprise. "The stable is an hour ahead of schedule. And I thought we were taking the coach-and-four, not the landau. The sturdy roof is less draughty for Aunt Havens."

"The landau is not for you. It's for me." He ripped a page from the journal and pressed it into her hand. "Something has come up with Parliament—"

"Something has come up with *Parliament?*" she repeated in derision. "They're not even meeting tonight. Will you be at the theatre in time for the performance?"

"I doubt it." He glanced over at the tiger who had just leapt down from the landau to open the door. "Forgive me, Katherine. This is important."

"'This is important,'" she mocked hollowly. Of course *his* plans mattered. But so did hers. "You have to be there. I need you. No one will donate money if they don't see you there doing the same, and Aunt Havens needs someone looking out for her now more than ever." She couldn't keep the panic from her voice. "I'm begging you to come. Please."

"Take my umbrella." He pushed the handle in her direction. "I must hurry. We'll talk tomorrow."

Her eyes stung. He didn't care about her event. He didn't even care about *her*. She might be a duchess, she might be his wife, but there were a thousand other strangers who would always take precedence. He would never choose her over duty.

"I think you know where you can stick that umbrella," she choked out, her voice thick.

He adjusted his top hat. "Katherine—"

She spun away before he could see how much he'd hurt her. "Go."

For a moment, for the briefest of heartbeats, he hesitated. And then he turned and climbed into the landau.

She stood in the rain, refusing to look at him, unable to move, as the carriage groaned back into motion and disappeared from sight.

Only then did she remember the torn page he'd thrust into her hand.

She glanced down at it with shaking fingers. The rain had streamed down her arm, coursing across the journal page in messy rivulets.

Most of the words had already washed away, but she could just make out the larger script of the title printed across the top:

A Poem For My Wife.

She pressed it to her chest in dawning horror and raced for the protective overhang covering the front steps.

Ravenwood had written her a poem.

He had finally worked up the courage to share it with her. Something she no doubt would have cherished forever.

And it was gone. Nothing more than a purple smear remained.

She leaned the back of her head against the brick of the house and stared bleakly at the stormy sky.

He would think she'd done it on purpose. He'd think she rejected his poem, rejected *him.*

When the truth was she would give her heart to have been able to read his words.

If she hadn't dallied for so long… If she'd paid attention when he'd given it to her… If she'd taken the blasted umbrella…

Heart breaking, she gazed numbly at the ink-stained page. There were no ifs.

The words were gone.

Chapter Twenty-Four

Kate tugged on a pair of too-tight gloves and strode from her bedchamber.

When she reached the front door, the butler stood at the ready with two umbrellas and two pelisses.

Aunt Havens was nowhere to be seen.

Kate didn't need to glance at her pocket watch to know they were running out of time. She needed to get there early. She needed to be there *now*.

With a sigh, she turned on her heel and made her way to the guest quarters.

Aunt Havens sat in the middle of the floor amongst a pile of spilled linens, playing with Jasper.

Kate tried very hard to keep her head from exploding.

"Aunt," she said with all the patience her heart could muster. "What in the world are you doing?"

"Playing," Aunt Havens replied joyfully. "I've just found a puppy."

Kate's mouth dried. Aunt Havens had been Aunt Havens a mere hour ago. And now…

"What is the puppy's name?" she asked thickly.

"He won't tell me," her aunt replied with a laugh. Her eyes widened as she glanced up at Kate. "You look lovely. Are you going somewhere?"

Guilt and indecision wracked her. She'd *promised* her aunt could attend tonight's gala.

She'd also promised hundreds of other attendees that the event would go off without a hitch. There was no possible way to manage the performances and patronages whilst simultaneously keeping a firm eye on Aunt Havens.

Not like this.

"No," she lied through the breaking of her heart. "I'm just...playing dress-up."

Aunt Havens smiled. "I love playing dress-up. I'll join you when I'm tired of the puppy."

Kate did her best to smile back. It wouldn't stay on her face.

"You stay here," she said instead. "Don't leave this room. I'll be back as soon as I can."

Aunt Havens frowned. "You *are* going somewhere!"

"Of course not," Kate managed. Her spine tightened with guilt. "I would never leave you. I just need you to stay right here until I come back."

Aunt Havens shrugged. "Suit yourself. I'm the one with the puppy."

Kate dropped to her knees and forced her aunt to meet her eyes. "Swear it. Tell me you won't leave this room until I come back to get you."

"I swear, sourpuss." Aunt Havens touched her nose to the puppy's. "Can I name him Bear?"

Kate tried to smile. "You should name him Jasper."

"Jasper," Aunt Havens repeated.

The puppy barked.

Aunt Havens laughed in delight. "He likes it!"

Kate pushed to her feet and met the worried eyes of Aunt Havens' lady's maid. "She stays in this room no matter what. Understood?"

The lady's maid nodded rapidly.

Kate kissed her aunt's wrinkled cheek. "I love you. Stay here."

Aunt Havens didn't answer.

Kate backed out of the room and then hurried toward the door. The gala was already a disaster. No Ravenwood. No Aunt Havens. No *Kate* if she didn't get out of this house and into the coach in the next few moments.

Her heart thumped as the carriage rattled toward the theatre. She felt awful for lying to Aunt Havens. Once she awoke from her confusion, she wouldn't even recall the conversation happening. All she would remember was that Kate had promised to bring her along then betrayed her by leaving her behind.

She desperately wished her last lucid moments with her aunt hadn't been spent fighting.

Rain beat down on the roof, on the windows, on the street. No pedestrians were outside. The cobblestones were buried beneath great puddles of mud.

When she arrived at the theatre, she had even less time to prepare than she'd feared. She rushed from one person to the next, encouraging performers, speaking to the staff.

Already guests were beginning to arrive.

Would they enjoy their experience? Would they even stay once they realized their sainted duke was not there?

Kate fought a sense of nausea. She had counted on Ravenwood's presence to motivate patronage and give a sense of aristocratic approval to the event. She feared his absence would convey the exact opposite message. That even *he* could not be bothered to support his wife's mad ideas.

Her body riddled with frustration. She had spent her adult life battling naysayers. People who believed a woman couldn't achieve things. People who believed communities like the one she was trying to build couldn't be achieved by anyone.

She had intended to prove them wrong.

It wouldn't be easy. There were a thousand interlocking parts to consider, most of them human and therefore utterly unpredictable. The countesses and earls were just as mercurial as the acrobats and opera singers. She had to be more than alert. For this to work, it had to be perfect.

The theatre filled to the rafters.

Kate's heart pounded.

Slowly, the curtain opened.

Music swelled as the orchestra began to play the opening for a skilled troupe of ballet dancers. Kate gripped her arms about her chest. The dancers leaped and twirled across the stage in time to the music. Every step, clockwork precision. Every leap, breathtaking.

The performance was flawless.

When it ended, the spellbound audience rose to their feet in applause. Kate could barely make herself heard when she walked on stage and asked them to please hold the applause until the end of the show, when they would all have an opportunity to speak with the performers themselves.

Next were the acrobats, the dramatists, the singers. Act after act, applause after applause. The audience couldn't help themselves. And Kate couldn't stop smiling. The first act was nearly over and the event was already a roaring success.

"Your grace?"

She turned to see the theatre manager hurrying toward her. "Yes?"

He wrung his hands apologetically. "There's a…gentleman here to see you. He says it's of utmost importance that he speak with you."

Kate's heart lifted. *Ravenwood*. No, that made no sense. The theatre manager wouldn't have referred to him as "a gentleman" but rather "his grace." And he would've shown Ravenwood to his seat immediately.

"I don't have time for interruptions." She gestured toward the stage. "I'm the one who has to cue each act, and it's almost time for the jugglers to take their bow."

A man stepped forward from the shadows. "My apologies, your grace. I would not have come if I hadn't felt it urgent."

"*Simmons?*" She stared at her butler in befuddlement. "What are you doing here?"

"It's Mrs. Havens," he said, his face pale. "She's gone."

"Gone?" Kate repeated stupidly. "How can Aunt Havens be gone?"

Simmons' eyes didn't quite meet hers. "The puppy got loose. He slipped outside and your aunt couldn't catch him and we all raced into the walking paths to find him before any harm could befall him. We were concentrating so hard on Jasper… It was dark as pitch and raining buckets, and we could barely see each other, much less the puppy. When we finally got him back inside, we discovered Mrs. Havens was gone."

"You found the puppy." Kate broke into a cold sweat. "And lost my aunt."

The butler's cheeks flushed with shame. "I take full responsibi—"

"I'm to blame," she interrupted, her stomach bottoming as terror took her. Aunt Havens was old and frail. And all alone. Somewhere.

Even from inside the theatre, the occasional crack of thunder could still be heard. The downpour was swift and merciless. Aunt Havens was in very real danger.

She searched frantically for her pelisse before remembering she'd left it at the other side of the theatre. There was no time. She had to find her aunt now before something terrible happened that couldn't be undone.

In a panic, she pushed past the butler and raced for the stairs. If anything happened to Aunt Havens…

"She promised she would stay home. Stay safe." Kate's voice cracked as she pushed out of the theatre and stepped into the driving rain. The carriage stood waiting, but Kate didn't even know where to begin to look. She stared up at the clouds. Aunt Havens was lost.

And it might be too late to find her.

Chapter Twenty-Five

Ravenwood entered White's with the memory of his wife's hurt seared into his brain.

He had given her the poem. It had taken hours to write. Days to finalize. Even if she found it puerile and laughable, she would at least know how much it had cost him to hand it to her. How much he loved her.

But it didn't mean she would forgive him for going back on his word.

He curled his fingers into fists and glared at the feather-brains who had ruined his night—and possibly his relationship—with their stupid obsession with seeing their faces on coins.

The problem with giving his word was that he had already given it. He was a duke. His first duty was to the Crown. To his country. That inherently meant everything and everyone had to come second. If he allowed these buffoons to ruin the economy, what kind of world he be making for his wife? For their children?

He had to do the right thing. But he'd be damned if he let it take all night.

Lord Montague rose to his feet as soon as he spotted Ravenwood striding through the door. "Gentlemen, gentlemen. As promised, the Duke of Ravenwood is here with incontrovertible proof to explain why the wisest decision, the *only* decision the Coinage Committee can make, is to reintroduce silver coins for denominations of forty shillings or less, establish a single gold standard for all transactions, and ensure a standard weight of all sovereigns relative to a twenty-two carat troy pound."

The moonfaced lords stared at Montague as if he were speaking Chinese. To them, it probably was.

That was the battle he and Ravenwood had been fighting since the beginning.

A battle Ravenwood intended to win right here.

Tonight.

He grabbed an empty tray from a passing servant and collected all the full and half-full glasses and snifters crowding the private table.

Ignoring all cries of *what's the meaning of this* and *you're not my headmaster, Ravenwood*, he handed the full tray off to a servant with instructions that no further beverages were to be served to any member of the current party without the Duke of Ravenwood's sole and express approbation.

Then he got to work.

For the next hour and a half, he and Montague slowly but surely turned the topic of England's fiduciary system from minting vainglorious fripperies to taking a solid look at the state of the economy and what changes might staunch the post-war slide, rather than exacerbate it.

He had never talked so much or so loudly. At first the others were startled into silence by his vociferousness and unyielding glare. Soon, however, the idea began to dawn in even the tiniest brains that the most diverting ideas for them was far from the best path for England.

Ravenwood stood at the head of the table, his face an implacable mask of ice. "It is your responsibility, your *duty*, to hold this country and every person in it in high esteem. My wife, my children, deserve to live in a stable world.

Where the value of a sovereign today is the same as it is tomorrow. So does your wife. So do your children. So do all of you."

They stared back at him, mouths agape.

"We are not only accountable for safeguarding the economy from further ravages. We are in the unique position of being powerful enough to ensure its stability for centuries to come."

They gazed at each other with a new kind of avarice.

Good. Ravenwood could use that to his advantage.

He placed both hands on the table and looked at each one in turn. "Do you want to be known as the dandies who put their faces on failing coins? Or do you want to be remembered as the peers who marshaled the resources of the House of Lords and restored England's position as the strongest economy in the world?"

In that moment, the damage was undone and the ridiculous coinage designs forgotten. No one wanted their face protruding from a mere penny when they could be immortalized as heroes instead. They would pass a Coinage Act focused on saving the economy, not their egos.

He was back in his landau within the next quarter hour.

It wasn't too late to attend Katherine's opening night. With luck, he might even arrive before the first intermission.

He squinted through the darkness. The streets were rivers due to the rain, but they were still passable. Particularly since few other drivers were out risking the storm.

Jaw set, Ravenwood pointed his landau toward the theatre.

And slowed the horses the moment he recognized yet another of his carriages standing near the main entrance. Why was his old chaise here? Had Katherine not come in the coach?

He grabbed his umbrella and leapt onto the wet road just in time to see his wife dash outside without so much as a pelisse to protect her from the pouring rain.

Cursing under his breath, he ran to her, his boots sloshing in the mud.

He swung the umbrella over her head and wrapped a dry arm about her shoulders. "What are you doing?"

"I have to go. We have to go," she said, her expression wild with panic. "Hurry!"

"Go where?" He stared at her. "Is your event over early?"

She turned glassy eyes to him. "I don't care about the gala. I have to find Aunt Havens."

The theatre door burst open behind them. To Ravenwood's shock, his butler raced outside.

"*Simmons?*" Ravenwood's ordered, logical brain could not think of a single sound reason for his butler to be at the theatre instead of home at his post. "What are you doing here?"

"We lost Mrs. Havens, your grace." Simmons' expression was grave. "I came to inform her grace. A few footmen are here with me, and the rest are out looking for Mrs. Havens."

The words were incomprehensible. Ravenwood swung his gaze to Katherine. "But isn't your aunt here with you?"

She stared up at him miserably. "I couldn't bring her. She was having an...an episode. I didn't want to risk something happening to her. I didn't want to risk..." She gave a short, half-hysterical laugh and shoved both he and his butler out of the way. "I have to get in the carriage. I have to find her. She needs me."

He wrapped an arm about her waist and pointed her toward his landau instead. "Come with me. We'll go together. Simmons, you follow."

The butler hesitated. "Where are we going?"

Ravenwood had absolutely no idea. "Where did you see her last?"

"At the house. The puppy got loose and—"

"You've searched for her near the estate for how long now?"

"A full hour."

"Then she's somewhere else." No wonder Katherine was frantic. Ravenwood tried to regulate his racing heartbeat. "She couldn't have gone far in the rain. It's hard enough for me to slosh through the current in these boots, let alone an older woman with a constitution like Mrs. Havens."

Katherine let out a hiccupy sob and bit down on her fist.

Ravenwood cursed his tongue. He hadn't meant to upset her further. He wanted to find her aunt, and the best tool at his disposal was his ability to reason. "Are any of the other carriages missing?"

Simmons shook his head. "I'm afraid not, your grace."

Ravenwood's chest tightened. "Even if there were any hack drivers on the road in this rain, she wouldn't have been able to hire one without coin to pay with."

"She always has money," Katherine said softly, her eyes wide with panic. "Aunt Havens says a lady should never be without pin money because a smart woman cannot always rely on someone else's pocketbook."

"She has money," Ravenwood repeated. Splendid. She could be anywhere. "Where might she go?"

"*Here*." Katherine's expression was bewildered and scared. "Straight here. She wanted to come to the gala. This is the only place she would go."

Ravenwood shot a sharp glance toward Simmons. "She's not inside? You checked?"

Simmons shook his head. "The ushers saw no one matching her description. Nor did anyone ask for her grace until I arrived."

Ravenwood's muscles stiffened. Losing Mrs. Havens felt like losing his own family. His knees weakened. She *was* his family. The same as Katherine. Guilt twisted his stomach. He should have been there, at Mrs. Havens' side.

Somehow they had to find her.

"She's not at home. And she's not here." Which left where, in this weather? She was unlikely to have stepped out for an ice, or a promenade in the park. His fingers began to shake. They would never find her if they couldn't figure out where to start looking.

"She wanted to come," Katherine whispered, eyes haunted. "She wanted to come and I wouldn't let her."

He grabbed her hands. "Think, darling. Where else might she go?"

"The maid was watching her. I even sent two footmen to keep her safe. I made her promise to stay home." Her voice fell to a whisper. "She probably didn't remember."

Ravenwood's mind clicked into place. "What if she went to another home?"

Katherine frowned up at him. "What?"

"Your townhouse. That was your home before you moved in with me. Might she have gone there?"

"I…" Katherine's eyes were wild. "It's closed up. I haven't been there in a month."

"Does she know that?" he insisted. "Does she remember?"

"There's no one there," Katherine stammered. "She doesn't have a key."

Blast. It had been the best he could come up with. "Is there no way to get inside? To seek shelter?"

Katherine shook her head. "Nothing short of climbing up the balcony to—" Her face paled. "Hurry!"

Ravenwood nodded at Simmons and swung Katherine up into the landau. He grabbed the reins and prayed harder than he ever had in his life that logic had failed him and he was wrong.

If Mrs. Havens had tried anything as foolish as climbing a balcony in her fragile condition…

They had to make haste.

Chapter Twenty-Six

Kate's old townhouse loomed beneath the storm-blackened sky, lit only by the occasional streak of white lightning. It looked empty. Barren.

Foreboding clogged her throat.

What if Aunt Havens was here, in the dark, in the rain? What if she were somewhere else entirely and they never found her?

Slowly, they drove around the townhouse. The front was closed up. The stoop bare. No signs of life, or even of a recent disturbance. Although if anyone had come by, their footprints would have long since washed away in the barrage of rain.

She gripped the edge of the squab and squinted through the sheets of rain as they rounded the corner toward the rear of the townhouse.

The high balcony was empty and dry. Its doors locked and undisturbed.

But there below, in the dark swamp of the grass, sat a thin, shaking form.

Aunt Havens.

Choking, Kate fumbled with the door and threw herself from the landau before it could even come to a stop.

She landed hard on her knees, hit the rocks instead of

the grass, but sprang up without feeling her torn skin and raced through the ankle-high mud.

"Aunt Havens!" she screamed. "Aunt Havens, I'm here! I came for you!"

The bent figure just kept trembling.

Kate slid in the mud, scrambled, kept going. She dropped to her knees and wrapped her arms about her aunt's cold, wet limbs.

Aunt Havens sneezed and kept shivering.

"You're going to be fine," Kate said softly, hugging her tight. "We'll get you home and get you warm. We're here now."

Footsteps splashed behind her as Ravenwood raced to her side. He pulled Aunt Havens up and into his arms.

Something white fluttered from her pelisse to the ground. Something small and familiar.

Kate scrambled to rescue the fallen scraps from the mud.

Her best evening gloves. The ones Aunt Havens had taken without asking. Each hand now boasted an intricately embroidered dahlia, exactly like the one Ravenwood had gifted Kate in his private garden.

The day she had told Aunt Havens she thought she might be falling in love.

Kate held it to her chest and tried not to sob. *The keepsake*. She'd fought with her aunt, yelled at her, accused her of not knowing her own mind... and all she'd been trying to do was give Kate something to remember her by.

She would wear them for the rest of her life.

Ravenwood nestled Aunt Havens in the landau. He covered her with the blanket and shucked off his greatcoat to give her added warmth.

Kate wrapped her arms about him and kissed him.

"You're freezing." She frowned. He was soaked to the bone. "You need to get dry, or you'll get sick, too."

He shook his head. "Don't worry about me. The important one is your aunt."

"You're both important. I won't risk anything happening to either of you."

She started to take off her pelisse.

He wouldn't let her.

"Stay warm," he ordered. Then sneezed. His hands shook as he held the reins. "We'll be home soon."

She hoped so. They *had* to. What if Ravenwood and Aunt Havens had both caught pneumonia?

Her throat tightened and she tried not to panic. "I'm never leaving either of you ever again."

As soon as they pulled up at Ravenwood House, she sent half the footmen to fetch surgeons and instructed the other half to help her turn Ravenwood and Aunt Havens' bedchambers into clean, warm sickrooms.

Because of her aunt's age, the surgeons didn't want anyone else present in Aunt Havens' sickroom. They suggested Kate go to her own bedchamber and try to rest.

She went straight to Ravenwood's.

"I'm fine," he said, despite wracking shivers. "Get some sleep."

"I'm a duchess," she reminded him as she warmed his hands in hers. "I do what I want."

He smiled. "Not 'a' duchess. *My* duchess."

"Yours forever." She crawled into bed beside him and wrapped him in her arms.

She loved him too much to ever let go.

Chapter Twenty-Seven

Ravenwood's head pounded. Morning. It must be morning. He felt like he'd been unconscious for days.

Slowly, he opened his eyes.

Katherine's blue eyes stared back at him.

"Good morning," he said in surprise.

She laced her fingers with his. "Good afternoon, darling. You slept for twelve hours."

He sat up in surprise. "How is your aunt?"

"Much better." She smiled. "Stable."

He stretched, testing his arms and legs, then rubbed the back of his head. Other than his pounding temples and an impending sneeze, he felt fine. "Why are you in here with me?"

"Where else would I be?" Her smile wobbled and she gripped his hand tighter. "I thought I'd lost you."

His heart skipped. "You won't lose me. You didn't."

"I *can't* lose you." She crawled into his arms and buried her face in his chest.

He stroked her hair and held her close.

After a long moment, she brought his hand to her lips, then sat up straight. "Your fingers are cold."

He raised his brows. The summer had been exceptionally cool. "Aren't yours?"

She slid out of bed and crossed over to his bell pull. "I'll ring for a bath. The hot water will do you good."

He rubbed his temples. "I'm fine, Katherine. There's no reason to be so concerned."

"Of course there is," she said softly. "You're every-thing."

He opened his mouth to correct her just as two footmen stepped into the room.

She turned toward the door to give him privacy.

"Wait," he said. "About your opening gala—"

"There's no opening," she interrupted. "I cancelled the society."

"You…what?" he stared at her blankly. "You are *passionate* about that society."

"I was. And I was foolish. I cannot facilitate something that ambitious whilst also doing my duty to you and my aunt. I shall stay here in Ravenwood House where I belong."

He blinked. Furthering the arts was not only her most cherished dream, she was truly making it happen. He couldn't imagine someone as strong as Katherine choosing to give up what she loved most in exchange for a life she never wanted.

"I hope I never implied that being my duchess would preclude outside hobbies," he said. "Much less giving up your dreams."

"You didn't have to imply. I learned the lesson quite vividly." She gave him a weak smile. "I give up."

"But what will happen to everyone interested in the Society of the Creative and Performing Arts?"

"Nothing will happen. They can find a new director. Or they can go back to real life." She took a deep breath. "As will I."

He frowned. "You mean to do what, then? Return to your museum?"

She shook her head. "I'm giving that up, too. I cannot be

a curator of antiquities and give my full attention to my family at the same time. So I choose my family. *Our* family. I don't need the museum."

While he couldn't fault her logic—when first they'd met, he had been very much of the opinion that a proper duchess should not have outside interests—he had long since discovered that Katherine's many and varied interests were what made her Katherine.

Any woman could do a reasonable job at minding a household, or do her duty to a title and bear the requisite number of children. Not every woman could do so whilst managing an antiquities museum and planning a multi-class community to celebrate London's creative and performing artists.

The last thing he wished to do was to change her. He was *proud* of her. Katherine's dreams and passions were not only what intrigued him most, they were the very sides of her character that had caused him to fall in love.

He'd told her so quite clearly in the poem he'd given her just before her gala.

"Did you already forget the words I wrote for you?" he asked softly.

She flinched and lowered her gaze. "I am sorry. I didn't get a chance to read them."

His smile faltered. Of course she had not. It had been dreadful timing. "Because you were en route to your event?"

Her eyes met his. "Because I was angry at you and I stood too long in the rain. By the time I realized what you had given me, the ink had already washed away. It's…gone. All of it."

His words of love had disappeared in the storm.

He nodded slowly, grateful for nearly thirty years practice of keeping an expressionless mask firmly in place. It wasn't her fault. It was his. If he had just attended the gala as promised, none of last night's events would have happened.

Before he could think of the right words to say, two more footmen arrived with buckets of hot water.

"I'll let you bathe," Katherine said. She blew him a kiss. "Keep warm while I check on Aunt Havens. I may stay with her for a little while, but I'll be back soon."

He let her go. He had no choice.

But after his bath, he returned not to his bed but to his office. He left his book of poetry where it was. It would be a long while before he would feel inspired to write verses again. In the meantime, the rest of the world had continued to march on.

He pulled the pile of unread correspondence toward him and began to open letters. Tonight was the Coinage Act vote in the House of Lords. Due to his intervention at White's, Ravenwood had no doubt the motion would pass with little opposition. He doubted he even needed to be there.

The letters that were not about impending recoinage wanted to start a pillory committee, or investigate slavery in the North African Barbary States. All were worthy causes. All wanted Ravenwood to lead the fight. None had any doubt that he was the right man for the job.

He drew a fresh sheet of paper and dipped his pen into the ink.

Katherine's words came back to him.

Time spent doing the things she loved necessarily meant time spent away from Ravenwood House. And so she'd chosen Ravenwood House.

She'd chosen *him*.

It might not have quite the same flourish as heart-wrenching lines of love poetry, but her decision was one that would never dissolve in the rain. His breath caught.

Every time any new issue arose in the House of Lords, he had always been the one to take on more than his share. He was a duke. He'd thought it his duty.

He set down his pen and flung the entire stack of correspondence into the fire.

One's duty could never be *more* than one's share. He would opine. He would attend meetings. He would vote. But he would never again put his family second.

He pushed to his feet, intending to tell Katherine right away. She didn't need to give up everything she wanted. They would meet in the middle. Make time for each other.

Then he remembered she was in the sickroom with her aunt. Not precisely the proper venue for discussing marital compromises. He would wait until she was free.

He quit the office, intending to walk out to his garden, but instead found himself entering the east wing of Ravenwood House. Toward the old family parlor.

It had been weeks since he'd ventured into these corridors. Weeks since his only connection to family was a cracked painting upon a wall.

As he approached the parlor, fading sunlight from the windows cast the room in an otherworldly pink glow. He stopped. His heart pounded in disbelief. The parlor was no longer empty.

He stared at the impossible transformation. The painting not only still hung upon the wall, it had been brought to life before his eyes.

He stepped forward slowly, scarcely daring to believe any of it was real. The tips of his fingers grazed the back of his mother's chaise, the arm of his father's hand-carved chair. He threw himself onto the floor as he'd done as a child when he would lay his head against his mother's cushion to listen to his father read.

Everything was exactly how it had been. Joy filled him. It was wonderful. It was perfect. He could hardly wait to tell Katherine—

But of course there could be no one else who could have wrought such a miracle. *She* did this for him. He didn't know how, but he knew she had done it.

Every cushion, every candelabra, every slope of the

painstakingly carved furniture were her words of poetry. Her lyrics and stanzas. Her way of showing him that he, too, was loved.

He needed to find her right now. Heart light, he strode from the room in search of his wife.

She was not with her aunt. The sickroom was quiet and dark. Evening had fallen. Katherine must have gone to bed. Light flickered in the crack beneath their adjoining door.

He knocked softly.

She didn't answer.

Frowning, he turned the handle and eased the door open a crack.

Katherine lay in the center of her bed, asleep. A forgotten taper still burned at her bedside.

He stepped inside and crossed the room as quietly as he could in order to blow out the candle. He halted just before he reached the bedside table when he spied the stained edge of a scrap of parchment protruding from beneath her pillow.

His poem.

He slipped it free.

She was right. It was nothing more than a blurry mess.

Yet she slept with it beneath her pillow. The rain-crinkled parchment was worn smooth from frequent handling, the crease lines transparent from being folded and unfolded so many times.

He swallowed. Even though it was ruined, she'd still tried to read it. She loved him too much to throw it away.

He slipped it back beneath her pillow and blew out the candle. But instead of returning to his bedroom, he strode back to his office.

Perhaps he was inspired to write poetry after all.

Chapter Twenty-Eight

Kate awoke to a cold, empty room.

She'd fallen asleep thinking about Ravenwood. The look on his face when she'd confessed to never even reading his poem… Her throat thickened.

She had been so focused on instilling greater understanding and appreciation for the beautiful, artistic world around her that she'd failed to apply the same dedication to her marriage.

Not anymore. She was Duchess of Ravenwood. From this day forward, she would embody that role with the same passion she held for antiquities and the arts.

No—with *more* passion. She would give her husband a real reason to be proud of her. Theatre was a fictional world. She lived in this one. Antiquities would not keep her warm at night or write poetry for her.

Only Ravenwood did that. With luck, he would someday do so again.

She rolled to her side and slid her hand beneath the pillow to retrieve the poem he'd written her. What was left of it, anyway.

The parchment crinkled and nicked the pad of her finger.

She frowned. The parchment was no longer stiff enough

to crinkle. She'd handled it too much, straining by candlelight to try and make out any words from the blurred soup. The paper was almost soft as linen.

Until now.

She shot upright and flung the pillow from the bed. It was not the same parchment at all. It was a fresh sheet, not torn from a journal or ravaged by rain. Folded into crisp thirds, it lay perfect and innocent right where the ruined poem had lain the night before.

She glanced at the closed connecting door separating her bedchamber from her husband's, then unfolded the parchment with trembling fingers.

A Second Poem For My Wife was printed in a now-familiar hand across the top of the page.

Her breath caught.

> *I once believed my heart an empty plain*
> *And seeded it with hope and loss and pain*
> *Flowers grew, and bristles, too*
> *But still the endless emptiness remained*

> *Until the day I looked into your eyes*
> *And saw that sun was more than just the sky*
> *You made me whole, a balm to my soul*
> *With you my heart could finally learn to fly*

Her fingers shook. He wasn't furious at her for letting the rain destroy his poem after all. That wonderful, gallant, unpredictable man had written her a new one—and delivered it while she slept.

Pulse racing, she trembled as she read the rest of the romantic words filling both sides of the paper. Every verse filled her heart even more. She read the lines again and again.

He loved her. Not for her beauty or grace, but for the

enthusiasm she held for everything around her. He loved her passion for antiquities, her fervent dream to unite artists and aficionados of all types.

But mostly, he loved how she loved. How she opened herself wholeheartedly, no matter how much it might hurt. How to be loved by her meant something true, deep, and unconditional.

How with her, he'd found his future...and lost his heart.

She gasped and pressed the poem to her chest. Her pulse pounded. She loved him so much she thought her heart might burst from the intensity.

She leapt up from the bed and burst through their adjoining door into his bedchamber.

It was empty.

She spun back to her dressing room and rang for her maid to help button her into a day dress as quickly as possible.

The moment she was presentable, she dashed from her chamber and raced straight for his office.

It was empty.

Frustrated, she tried the library, the dining rooms, then finally found him in her aunt's sickroom, reading aloud to Aunt Havens from an Ann Radcliffe gothic novel. Her heart swelled.

He rose to his feet the moment he saw her.

She flew across the room and into his arms. "I'll make you the best possible duchess Ravenwood House has ever seen."

"I *have* the perfect duchess," he said in his low voice as he held her tight. "I saw the family room. I have no idea how you did it, but...thank you. You're amazing."

Warmth spread through her. "I wanted you to have more than memories. I wanted you to have a piece of your family."

"*You* are my family," he told her. "You, Aunt Havens, Jasper... We are a family. Together. That parlor is more than a miracle. It's meant to be enjoyed. By all of us. We'll fill it with new memories."

She smiled into his cravat and snuggled close. "I love you."

"I love you, too." He lifted up her chin with his knuckle. "And I'd like you to rethink your resignation from the Society of the Creative and Performing Arts."

She rose on her toes to kiss him. "I can't go anywhere. Perhaps, once Ravenwood House once again runs smooth as clockwork…"

He arched his brows. "And perhaps you don't have to go anywhere at all."

She frowned up at him in confusion.

His grin was slow and wicked.

"Your grace?" The butler appeared in the doorway. "Guests are beginning to arrive."

"Guests?" she asked, baffled. He'd invited people over while she slept?

"Send them to the ballroom," Ravenwood ordered. "I believe they'll all fit."

"Ballroom?" she repeated. "At ten o'clock in the morning?"

The last time the Ravenwood ballroom had been used was seven months ago, when Lady Amelia had requisitioned it as a replacement venue for the seventy-fifth annual Sheffield Christmastide ball. Kate was certain her husband had only attended because it was his sister and his house.

"What on earth is happening?" she demanded.

He lifted a shoulder. "Your gala was cut short when you didn't return after intermission. The performers and the patrons never received their promised opportunity to meet as equals, nor to discuss the arts or potential sponsorship."

"You invited them here?" Giddiness made her light-headed. "To the Ravenwood ballroom?"

"Our ballroom," he corrected. "It should be large enough to serve as a monthly gathering point until you are ready to organize a supplementary gala for the second half of the performance. If the post is any indication, it will be an even worse crush than the opening night."

"You're helping with the gala?" She stared at him in befuddlement.

He shook his head. "Not just the gala. I am offering my services in any capacity you might need. There's no reason to give up your dream. We can work on it together. You'll just have to show me how." He narrowed his eyes. "But please don't make me memorize any journals."

"Done." Laughing, she pressed her lips to his.

The Society for Creative and Performing Arts wouldn't just be a success for others—it would ensure she and her husband had even more reasons to spend time together. A mutual passion. They would be a team.

She laced her arms about his neck. "Have I mentioned how much I love you?"

"How fortuitous." He swung her into his arms. "After the meeting, you can show me."

She laughed and smacked his shoulder. "I intend to show you how much I love you every single day."

He kissed her back. "As do I, my love. As do I."

Epilogue

Ravenwood set his pen back in the standish and looked up from his poetry. The family parlor looked much the same as it had during his childhood—with a few notable exceptions.

The vase at the window no longer held traditional English roses, but rather a single exotic dahlia, plucked fresh from his garden.

Ravenwood's new writing desk near the fireplace was a gift from his wife, and had been hand-carved in the same style as his father's favorite chair.

A chair which, at this moment, was occupied by Katherine's Aunt Havens, whose attempts at embroidering a blanket for the new baby kept being interrupted by the much larger but equally rambunctious Jasper knocking over the embroidery basket.

"Dreadful beast," Aunt Havens scolded with an indulgent smile.

Jasper was too busy gnawing on balls of thread to notice.

Katherine reclined on the chaise longue with their son snuggled up against the protruding bulge of her belly, as they leafed through a sketchbook of flowers, commenting on which ones they'd seen in the parks or on one of their many family picnics in Papa's special garden.

In a few weeks, Parliament would come back into session and the London Season would once again be well underway.

Ravenwood would not be joining any committees this year. Not only did he and his wife have the fourth annual Society of Creative and Performing Arts opening gala to plan, he'd much rather be home with his family than cooped up in the Palace of Westminster.

Contentment coursing through him, he scooped Jasper out of Aunt Havens' embroidery basket and nestled on the chaise next to his wife and child. The old parlor was finally a family room again. For the first time in decades, he no longer needed to yearn for what the future might hold.

He had everything he could ever want right here.

The End

Thank You For Reading

I hope you enjoyed this story!

Sign up at EricaRidley.com/club99
for members-only freebies
and special deals for 99 cents!

**Did you know there are more
books in this series?**

This romance is part of
the *Dukes of War*
regency-set historical series.

Join the *Dukes of War* Facebook group for
giveaways and exclusive content:
http://facebook.com/groups/DukesOfWar

In order, the Dukes of War books are:

The Viscount's Christmas Temptation
The Earl's Defiant Wallflower
The Captain's Bluestocking Mistress
The Major's Faux Fiancée
The Brigadier's Runaway Bride
The Pirate's Tempting Stowaway
The Duke's Accidental Wife

**Other Romance Novels
by Erica Ridley:**

Let It Snow
Dark Surrender

About the Author

Erica Ridley is a *USA Today* bestselling author of historical romance novels. Her latest series, The Dukes of War, features roguish peers and dashing war heroes who return from battle only to be thrust into the splendor and madness of Regency England.

When not reading or writing romances, Erica can be found riding camels in Africa, zip-lining through rainforests in Central America, or getting hopelessly lost in the middle of Budapest.

For more information, please visit www.EricaRidley.com.

Acknowledgments

As always, I could not have written this book without the invaluable support of my critique partners. Huge thanks go out to Emma Locke and Morgan Edens for their advice and encouragement.

I also want to thank my incredible street team (the Light-Skirts Brigade rocks!!) and all the readers in the Dukes of War facebook group. Your enthusiasm makes the romance happen.

Thank you so much!

CPSIA information can be obtained
at www.ICGtesting.com
Printed in the USA
LVOW12s1802040516

486686LV00006B/423/P